VERA, or FAITH

GARY SHTEYNGART

Atlantic Books
London

First published in the United States in 2025 by Random House, an imprint and division of Penguin Random House LLC, New York.

First published in hardback in Great Britain in 2025 by Atlantic Books, an imprint of Atlantic Books Ltd.

10 9 8 7 6 5 4 3 2 1

A CIP catalogue record for this book is available from the British Library.

Hardback ISBN: 978 1 83895 880 0
Trade Paperback ISBN: 978 1 83895 881 7
E-book ISBN: 978 1 83895 882 4

Printed and bound by CPI (UK) Ltd, Croydon CR0 4YY

Atlantic Books
An imprint of Atlantic Books Ltd
Ormond House
26–27 Boswell Street
London
WC1N 3JZ
www.atlantic-books.co.uk

Product safety EU representative: Authorised Rep Compliance Ltd., Ground Floor, 71 Lower Baggot Street, Dublin, D02 P593, Ireland. www.arccompliance.com

In memory of Paul La Farge
and Rebecca Godfrey

Part One

•

The First Day

1.

She Had to Hold the Family Together

School started and it was awful. "Predictably awful," as Anne Mom would say. "A self-fulfilling prophecy" she might add of Vera's disdain for school. Anne Mom was always predicting things in the near future. "I'm the Nostradamus of two weeks from now," she told Vera over and over again and Vera knew the correct social response was to laugh because Anne Mom was trying to be as witty as Daddy, though when Vera became a teenager in three years she could roll her eyes, because she had seen it done on television and sometimes on the devices Anne Mom didn't allow her.

She added "Nostradamus" to her *Things I Still Need to Know Diary*.

The hallways of the school were a faded red and pink and orange and there were motivational posters and funny sayings from the Peanuts gang and dusty green floors and mesh over the windows looking onto the rump of another sad uptown building. Daddy compared the color scheme to an "ice-cream shop in hell" and Anne Mom had yelled at him not to use that language ("You know she's going to imitate you, she *worships* you!") or to talk the school down. The school was a point of pride for Daddy because you had to take a test when you were only four years old to get in, and you needed to score "in the ninety-ninth percentile," although Vera had overheard that Dylan had been admitted because they wanted to keep siblings together and she thought this contrast between their intelligence to be "exquisite" and "delectable," two words Anne Mom wanted her to drop if she were to make any friends at her school.

"Both my kids go to a public school," Daddy had once declared on television with what Anne Mom called a "raffish" smile while some other men in suits and ties were yelling at him about his "politics," although he had failed to mention that it was a school for superbright kids, and that made her sad. There were a lot of "statuses" in the world and each year she was becoming aware of more of them. For example, it also made her sad when Daddy sat apart from them on planes because he always had a ticket in "Business Class" and just this summer when they had flown to Korea and Japan, where Daddy had to deliver some speeches, she had asked him "Why can't you fly with us in Family Class?" and he said "Awwww, poor Doxie" (despite being short, she was shaped lean and tubular like a dachshund), then bent down and grizzled her forehead with his stubble and it hurt the whole ride back and she didn't see "a lick" (Anne Mom phrasing) of him for fourteen hours straight—not that she saw that much of him at home.

⸲

So, yes, school was predictably awful and a lot of it was dumb. Vera looked through the mesh on the windows at the Black people across the block who patronized a fish store. Sometimes they would look back at her and sometimes they would smile, maybe remembering how boring fifth grade had been. There was a lot of "advanced" work, but Vera breezed through it; mostly it was ordering things in rows and columns and sometimes demonstrating "comprehension." This year, because of the conventions, there was going to be a whole module on the Constitution and just how it might be amended.

All the students sat dutifully in their red checkered uniforms (the girls had to wear bow ties and skirts, the boys sweaters and ties) and raised their hands whether they knew an answer or not because participation was forty percent of their grade. There was only one troublemaker in the class, Stephen, one of the Moncler Twins (Anne Mom had named them thus because of the expensive winter jackets they wore), and he probably thought he could get away with it because he was Five-Three, same as Dylan and

Anne Mom, and both of the twins' parents were "super white" and could trace their heritage to the Revolutionary War. At least half the kids in her school were Asian or half Asian like Vera was, at least genetically because of her mom mom, who had been Daddy's girlfriend before he met Anne Mom. Mom Mom had abandoned her and Daddy, maybe because she didn't love Vera on account of that she had been a "tough baby" who couldn't go to sleep unless you drove her around the block in a car, and back then Daddy could barely afford the gas.

❦

It was said by both her pediatrician and her psychologist that Vera, while presenting as a very bright ten-year-old, suffered from intense anxiety, in the same way the rest of her family did except for Dylan, whose blond curls were constantly in motion as he made short work of the school's jungle gym and wrestled on the hot tarmac with his little buddies. School made her anxious, especially because of what Anne Mom called the "social component," but she had been worried the entire summer as well.

Her parents fought every day on a variety of subjects, but especially about how she and Dylan were to be raised. Anne Mom wanted a lot of structure, but Daddy said childhood "should just happen," like it had happened to him, and that until you went to grad school "nothing really mattered," it was all just a "neoliberal frog-march of the damned." (Daddy supplied a lot of the words for her *Things I Still Need to Know Diary*.) Once, she even overheard him crying in "Daddy's Little Pool" as she used to call the hot tub at their summer house when she was much younger and more innocent, and she begged Anne Mom to please not fight with him anymore that day. But Anne Mom told her that Daddy was crying because someone important—the "Rhodesian Billionaire" who wanted to buy his magazine and thus make them "more comfortable"—had been especially mean to him on social media and that he felt bullied. "If he's being bullied he should talk to someone," Vera told Anne Mom, but Daddy kept crying softly like one of the wounded wild animals in the forest behind the hot tub and nothing could be done about it until dinner and time for his first glass of what she used to call "Daddy's mar-tiny," or if he went straight to wine, "Daddy's special juice."

She tried to "dialogue" with Dylan about their family situation, but he would just go on playing with his robot dinos on the porch while their summer house shuddered with their parents' elegant and vicious turns of phrase. "Don't you care if they get divorced?" she would whisper to Dylan, even though no one was in earshot, because the words felt so sad and shameful to her. Her love for Anne Mom was measured, but to have two moms leave her (surely, she would take Dylan with her in the split) would mean she was beyond loving, beyond Family Class. "I dunn ah"—Dylan would shrug and then punch her in the elbow where it hurt the most. "Fine, but don't come to me when we're homeless," Vera told him.

Becoming homeless worried Vera. She read the billboards at the bus shelters very earnestly. One told her that sixty-three percent of the occupants of homeless shelters in the city were members of families, probably failed families like her own would become if she were unable to hold her parents together, or if her daddy didn't manage to sell the troubled magazine he edited to the Rhodesian Billionaire who would make them comfortable and unafraid. She had once quizzed her dad on the subject of their finances, and he had said, "Well, we're not poor, but we're not superrich like half the jerks in this city."

"Then what are we exactly?" Vera had asked. She liked to be exact.

"We're what's called merely rich," Daddy explained, "but our position is very precarious especially with how much I've staked on this goddamn magazine. We could lose everything, and your mother's trust just pays for the incidentals. Unless we moved to a small metro in the sticks. And then I'd like to see your mom eat a plate of General Tso's chicken or whatever."

So, it was true, she thought. They were all going to end up in a homeless shelter. Especially if Daddy's magazine remained unsold "and/or" Daddy and Anne Mom got divorced.

"Ergo," another diary word, she had to hold them together.

Ergo, the Lists.

,

She composed the first List during math, which was such an easy subject she could do it seemingly with just her eyes and hands, her brain concentrating on more important tasks. She had lost so many points over the years for not showing her work, which made Anne Mom sigh, because the "means are every bit as important as the ends" or something "Protestant" like that, as Daddy would say. The only math that truly stimulated her was the module on imaginary numbers last year, because she found the concept so beautiful. Here and not here, like the feathery touch of Daddy's hand when he petted her and not Dylan, to whose pallor he gravitated more and more as her brother's raffish personality filled out. Miss Campari, the math teacher, had what Anne Mom would call a "pendulous bosom," something she said with enough laughter to shake her own smaller one. "Mommy's humor is still stranded somewhere in the twentieth century," Daddy would say over a pendulous glass of his "special juice." She couldn't help but stare at it as it moved around the room, past all those bow-tied girls and boys, so focused and obedient and bored, except Moncler Stephen, who would yawn dramatically and make everyone else laugh and shrug off his reprimand with a shake of his beautiful hair.

The first List would be addressed to Anne Mom, so she had to write it in her best handwriting, which was usually clustered and unreadable like a boy's. "The only way you and Dylan are at all alike," Anne had said of her scribbles, which made her treasure her "crappy" (bad word) penmanship and want to improve it all at once.

Ten Great Things About Daddy and Why You Should Stay Together with Him

1. He's an intellectual.
2. Is on TV sometimes.
3. Has been long-listed for many prizes in the United Kingdom (aka England after Scotland and the rest of them left).
4. Edits a magazine for smarties.
5. Is funny most of the time.
6. Looks raffish in his tuxedo when he has to go to a benefit.
7. Lets us tag along on many ~~delectable~~ fascinating trips.
8. Survived his parents and immigration, so can survive anything.

9. Speaks two languages.
10. His long struggle for full recognition is about to be over.

She looked over the List. It was pretty good and it mostly used Anne Mom's nicest words about Daddy. Anne Mom had often said that instead of talking to girls her age using her own thoughts she should listen to them and try to repeat the things that most excited them. The technique was called "mirroring" and even spies used it! Yes, it was a great List and it really captured the "point of Daddy."

Now she had to embark upon a far-greater challenge.

Ten Great Things About Mom and *Why You Should Stay with Her*

1. Maintains her beauty.
2. Has a "non-waist."
3. Has a "little trust."
4. Went to Brown for graduate school.
5. Makes a lot of delectable "WASP lunches" for all of us.
6. Is Five-Three which will keep us safe.

That was all she could think of, so she crossed out the "Ten" in "Ten Great Things About Mom" and made it

"Six." Six was enough and an even number. According to Anne Mom, there was no point in being odd "all the time."

She felt Miss Campari's bosom approach her from behind and sucked in her breath, preparing to be smart so she could "advance in the world." Often when she felt like she couldn't breathe, her hand found the center of the clip-on bow tie and she pulled on it as if it were the string of a windup toy.

The bell rang.

2.

She Had to Survive Recess

She always looked forward to recess until it started. She just wanted to move her body. She went into a bathroom stall and shook out her hands. Over and over, she shook them out, until they were a complete blur and her mind went elsewhere, to the much-maligned Korean province of Jeolla where Mom Mom was from and which they didn't visit on their trip to Korea; to the place where "warm liquid flows into your body from the top of your head until it fills you up," as Anne Mom's meditation app had taught her; to the slurred nonabsence of Daddy after a few mar-tinys as his hand magically found its way around Ann Mom's non-waist and it seemed like the marriage would hold through the week and maybe they would all be okay. Shaking out her hands was the thing Anne Mom hated the most and even Daddy raised one of his oversize eyebrows when she did it. "Stop flapping," Anne Mom would say. "You're annoying everyone." "I'm not *flapping*,

I'm not a seal," Vera would say. "I'm shaking out my excess energy." But she couldn't shake it out forever and after a few minutes her shoulders hurt so she went out onto the playground with her book.

The sunlight was brutal and the hairs on her tired arms—"your daddy's genetic gift"—were soon coated with a shimmer of liquid. It was, as Daddy liked to say, "perfect nine-eleven weather," but she didn't think it perfect at all. There were only three benches and the girls usually took all of them while the boys ran around in mad circles colliding with one another and screaming in pain, which sometimes led to laughter. One of the nice girls, Yumi from Japan, always saved a tiny space on the edge of a bench for Vera to sit with her book, but then she would turn her back to her to talk to the Populars. They were talking loudly about their summers and all the different camps they had been sent to, algebra camp, violin camp, Cantonese camp. Sometimes they'd watch the boys, especially Moncler Stephen and her brother, Dylan, who were taking turns slapping each other by the jungle gym, even though they were two grades apart. "They're so stupid," the girls would say, but then for some reason keep staring at Stephen. Maybe Vera knew the reason, because even though she hated Stephen, hated the disorder he brought to class (she just wanted to get through the work and go home), she stared at him, too.

She thought of putting down her book on chess strategies and talking to the girls about her own summer, which, frankly, had been so much more interesting than violin camp. But what could she say? How to start the conversation? Anne Mom had always prodded her to make a friend of Yumi, whose parents were diplomats from Japan and according to Daddy "super cultured." Now that she had been to Japan, maybe she could say something. *We were on the Shinkansen, which is the bullet train, and I got super scared because the screen said there was a typhoon that was going to hit Okinawa and we were headed in that direction, to Kyoto to see the five temples.* But she could already hear Anne Mom's critique. *You don't have to tell her the Shinkansen is the bullet train. She's from Japan. She knows. Think of your audience. And why start with how you were scared. Mention something incredible you saw or a fabulous meal you had.*

Think of your audience. That was something Daddy did the best and he had so many friends around the world and now he was running an old magazine people had completely forgotten about until Daddy took it over (although it was very hard to get them to pay to read it), and now the Rhodesian Billionaire was "angling" to buy it. When he got the job, they had to throw out all the tote bags with the names of other magazines especially the one for the "magazine of record" as Daddy dismissed it, the one she saw all over town.

Shinkansen, five temples, "Damn [bad word], this soba is freaking [probably bad word] amazing," no typhoon, no typhoon. But she couldn't say anything; sweet Yumi started laughing hard about something, and now it was too late to "butt in." She could feel the warmth of Yumi's shuddering back against her shoulder, against the tiny hairs of her arm. How lucky Yumi's little sister was to have someone like her to look up to. "Someone will love you in college," Anne Mom had once told her. "You'll have friends and maybe even a boyfriend or a girlfriend." Yes, Vera had said, but what about now? Not the boyfriend or girlfriend part, but a friend.

She took *The Chess Player's Bible* and walked around the jungle gym to witness the simplicity of her brother. Why did she have to talk to girls instead of running after them or trying to tackle them to the ground? She could play with Dylan—he would always let her into his throbbing social life if only to get a chance to pinch or slap her—but then she would be playing with her younger brother, which would probably be "pathetic," a word Daddy used, according to Anne Mom, with "particular relish," which made Vera think of the delicious hot dog they had eaten in Tokyo made out of fried potatoes and soy skins. Maybe that's how she could have started a conversation with Yumi! *Think of your audience.*

But it was too late, as she was behind the jungle gym fence separating the school from the neighborhood in which it found itself, and her arms were shaking, shaking, shaking, not flapping, nothing like a seal, she just wanted to let the energy out, she just wanted the day to be over, and to see the two friends she really had, Aunt Cecile, who was not really her aunt but who would be over for dinner—which meant her parents would have to be on their best behavior—and Kaspie the Chess Computer with whom she shared her room. She saw some Black church ladies with their tall lavender hats standing on the corner beyond the fence passing out their "literature," though Daddy had a thick opinion of what constituted the same. When they went to someone's house she and Dylan made a game of seeing if they had a copy of an enormous book called *The Power Broker* and whether or not its spine had been cracked and then Daddy would give each of them a dollar for the information.

The women had a stand for their literature, with a drawing of a woman who looked remarkably like Anne Mom holding her head in pain the way she actually did before she took Vera and Dylan to get "Mommy's special vitamins" at the drugstore. No, it was really remarkable how they had gotten Anne Mom just right, the long frosted squiggles of her blond hair, the sharp nose that ran down and then curled up like a ski jump, and the dimple of a chin clenched in pain. WILL SUFFERING END? the sign read. Yeah, Vera thought, *will it?*

Nothing was as pleasant as hearing the gym teacher Mr. Garnetti blow the whistle to signal that recess was over and the remains of the school day were set to begin. Only three hours left and after that two hundred and three school days until summer began again. Maybe next year, if they still had the money and weren't homeless, they could go see Jeolla and she could walk past the giant terraced plains that entombed her ancestors, where part of her story began, before she became a bad baby who couldn't sleep (not that she had much success sleeping now) and Mom Mom couldn't take it anymore and left.

❦

Instead, Vera walked to her classroom past the "mimeograph room," whatever that was (Daddy, taking a photo of the sign: "I just can't believe this place"). She examined the grimy fire extinguisher, worried that it was too "effed up" (unspeakable word, for internal use only) to save the school from an inferno, but got a "That's not for kids!" from Ron the Guard upon touching it. She sighed. Being a kid sucked, a word Anne Mom permitted in small quantities, especially if Dylan used it with his cute, hoarse little voice.

Ms. Tedeschi was a popular young teacher who seemed to wear sundresses well into the winter. She taught social studies and had been Vera's teacher last year and she always laughed (in a good way) at the scope of Vera's vocabulary. Vera and the other kids listened to Ms. Tedeschi, their eyes hard in concentration, because everyone knew Ms. Tedeschi was worth listening to. "A fine educator," Anne Mom had said of her, and Daddy had grunted.

Ms. Tedeschi spoke of the importance of kids being "in the know." "I hate calling you 'kids,'" she said, "because in times like these, you have to grow up fast." Vera smiled at this—she wanted to grow up superfast. It's like Ms. Tedeschi was mirroring her thoughts. She sure "knew her audience." No wonder everyone loved her. She was like Aunt Cecile if Aunt Cecile was an educator in sundresses instead of an actor in tight jeans. "This is one of the most consequential years in the history of our country," Ms. Tedeschi said. "Does anyone know the meaning of 'consequential'?" All the hands shot up except for Stephen's and the new boy from Taiwan, who passed the test to get into the school but still needed to work on his English. Ms. Tedeschi's grades did not give forty percent for participation, it was hard to figure out what her grading system was, but (almost) everyone wanted to participate nonetheless. "Significant," Yumi said, once called upon. "Important."

"Also, 'following something as a result,'" Vera said.

"Very good, Vera, but please wait to be called on."

Vera managed to smile and frown at the same time using her nose and eyebrows, a Daddy trick. "It's a consequential year," Ms. Tedeschi said, "because the states are having their constitutional conventions. And these conventions will decide whether to give an 'enhanced vote'"—she made the quotation marks with her long fingers—"counting for five-thirds of a regular vote to so-called 'exceptional Americans,' those who landed on the shores of our continent before or during the Revolutionary War but were exceptional enough not to arrive in chains." Half the room turned to face Stephen, who was picking something out from the crux of his elbow, hardened dirt or a scab maybe, his forehead consumed with the effort.

Vera wanted to say that Anne Mom was holding a fundraiser against Five-Three next week, that would be mirroring Ms. Tedeschi, except maybe Ms. Tedeschi liked Five-Three and had a thing for "exceptional Americans" like Stephen. One technique Daddy had tried to teach her—with Anne Mom's explicit approval—was how to pick up on "tone of voice" and, Daddy's own God-given specialty, sarcasm. Vera kept her hand down.

"But we're not just mindless puppets," Ms. Tedeschi said, her black eyes skirting the windows as if sucking in the endless late-summer light of the outside world. (Vera loved black holes, but was also reasonably scared of them.) "We're still participants in our country's destiny and we still have a voice." Yeah, but kids can't vote, Vera wanted to say. But she knew not to be negative when Ms. Tedeschi sounded so positive. "So this module, we'll be doing what has historically been called a Lincoln–Douglas debate. Does everyone know who Abraham Lincoln was?" Everyone knew. Even the new Taiwanese kid thrust his hand in the air like he wanted to punch the sky. After a penny and a five-dollar bill were produced (the latter from Stephen, who besides his Moncler jacket clearly had quite the allowance), the less exceptional personage of Senator Stephen Douglas was duly explained.

"So I'm going to start by picking two of you to be the primary debaters," Ms. Tedeschi said, "and then I'll pick two to be part of your teams and to be alternates in case you can't fulfill your duties." The kids murmured in delight. When Ms. Tedeschi used adult vocabulary without explanation, it made them feel even more important. "Since Lincoln debated Stephen Douglas and we actually have a *Stephen* in the room"—there was some laughter—"Stephen Wilson, you will take the position against Five-Three." Vera heard "Whoa!" from a couple of kids and almost uttered it herself. Why would Stephen of all the students in the class be against Five-Three? "Davis Yang"—this was the Taiwanese boy—"will be your alternate."

"Whoa," Stephen said. "That sounds sketch. He's not even American." The Populars who liked Stephen rolled their eyes, but Vera knew they liked him still. She rolled her eyes as well, though no one was looking at her.

"That may be," Ms. Tedeschi said, "but you will have to rely on him if you have any hope of winning. The primary debater for the *pro*-Five-Three side will be Vera Bradford-Shmulkin."

Vera brought her hand to her bow tie and pulled on its center. She needed her thoughts to line up in an orderly fashion. She wanted to say something funny and cool and maybe with a touch of eye roll. "That's delectable!" she cried out. The kids laughed predictably, but she almost didn't mind. Wait until Anne Mom found out she was debating *pro*-Five-Three. When Ms. Tedeschi announced that Yumi from Japan would be her alternate, Vera turned back and looked at her with what she didn't know were her most loving eyes ("I like your tender side, Doxie," Daddy would say when they occasionally curled up next to each other on the living room couch after a long day "at the salt mines") and got a Yumi smile and a shrug in return. "Remember to listen and be kind to your teammate," Ms. Tedeschi said, primarily to Stephen, but Vera nodded seriously at this injunction.

She had, if not a friend, a teammate.

When the bell rang she wanted to rush over to her and tell her about the Japanese hot dog right away. *Take it easy,* she heard Anne Mom saying. *Take it easy.*

3.

She Had to Get Through the
March of the Hated

Their car shot down the highway, Vera counting streets in the back seat, hoping they would match up with the exit signs when they passed them. "Ninety-six," she said out loud, pleased to have counted correctly.

She felt the pain in her elbow, particularly sharp today as it was delivered with the cruelest aim. "Octagon!" Dylan yelled.

"Ouch!" Vera yelled back.

"Dylan," Anne Mom said, softly. She was up front with one hand on the bottom of the steering wheel and the other hand on her aching head. Stella the Car was doing the driving.

"We have an agreement," Dylan whined. "Whoever sees the Octagon first gets to punch the other one." The

Octagon was a building on an island in the middle of the river.

"Yes, but maybe not so hard," Anne Mom said. "Seriously, I don't feel well today. Don't make me come back there."

"There is a March of the Hated on our avenue today," Stella announced in her sonorous voice. (That maybe wasn't the right word, but Vera loved the word "sonorous," loved its musicality.) "Should I take the backstreet to let you off in the basement and find a different garage to park in?"

"No!" Dylan shouted. "I wanna see the march! I wanna see those losers!"

"They're not losers, they're just confused," Vera said, repeating someone she might have heard on one of the TV programs with Daddy.

"You know your sister can't get to sleep when she sees a march," Anne Mom said, her hand gripping the wheel she wasn't turning.

"'Cause she's the loser!" Dylan shouted.

"Dylan," Anne Mom said. "I'm so tired today. I'm so very tired."

When Anne Mom used the word "very" they both knew to shut up.

Dylan leaned over to Vera, his curls on her shoulder, and whispered "I hate you" with his Cheetos breath.

Right back at you, she mouthed. *You wouldn't even be in our special school without me,* she wanted to say.

Dylan had run straight up to the police barricades at the last March of the Hated and made funny faces at the marchers. Some of the policemen laughed even though Daddy said most of them were pro-Five-Three.

Vera didn't know why the MOTH upset her so much. Well, she knew and she didn't know. It definitely *sucked* (how thrilling to keep thinking that word!) that it happened on the avenue around the corner from their building and that it happened almost every week now that the conventions were drawing near.

But what sucked more were the kids they had marching. The way the MOTHs were arranged these days, first you had the police cars with their sirens wailing a staccato of "whoop whoop!" punctuated by even-scarier silence. Then you had the first marchers beneath a sign that read BLACKS FOR 5/3. Behind them were the "Hasidics" as Daddy called them with the sign that read PIOUS JEWS FOR 5/3. Vera did not fully understand why Blacks and Jews, who, from everything she had read, probably couldn't trace their heritage to the Revolutionary War, would be in these marches, but what really "broke her heart" (a phrase from a book she read last year which made her imagine the left and right ventricles lying on one side and the left and right atriums on the other, pining desperately for one another) were the teenage and even-younger white kids marching in their dirty mechanic's and farm overalls with the sign THEY HAVE TAKEN MY FUTURE AWAY FROM ME.

The adult counterprotesters behind the police barri-cades always went nuts when these kids walked by. They would shout "Stop exploiting your kids!" or some ver-sion of that, even though it was difficult to say whom (not "who") they were shouting at. When she asked Daddy what the sign meant, he said that "they" was a clever reference to the Hasidics marching ahead of the "benighted white working-class kids," a "classic trope" according to Daddy (the word "trope" headlined her *Things I Still Need to Know Diary*). But that made no sense and she had to get this right for her debate if Yumi were to become her friend.

But more than anything she felt sorry for these kids. *Heartbroken.* Two ventricles here, two atriums there. They looked even sadder than she sometimes felt during recess, their eyes to the ground, some of their faces smeared with dirt, their futures gone, even though presumably they were all Five-Three and could vote "exceptionally" once they turned eighteen. No, she couldn't sleep alone to-night, especially if the sounds of the MOTH reverberated past their windows.

"I'm so tired," Stella the Car said, mimicking Anne Mom, as she dropped them off by the basement entrance on the other side of their building. Stella "knew her audience" (Anne Mom) and the mirroring technique well.

,

"Daddy! Daddy!" Vera and Dylan shouted as Anne Mom opened the door to the apartment.

"Dyl-man. Doxie," Daddy said. He was on the big gray couch in his underwear, doing social media on his phone. Vera could tell because his mouth was open. "Social media work *is* work," he would say whenever Anne would chide him for being "absent" to his kids. "It's what keeps the lights on around here."

The kids crowded around Daddy and pressed themselves into his chest hair, which Vera thought looked like the Nile River delta. Daddy lifted up his phone to see it better over them. "Can you ask them how their first day of school was?" Anne Mom said as she removed the remains of their lunches from their backpacks and set out their homework.

"How was your first day of school," Daddy said, forgetting the question mark.

"Good?" Vera said.

Dylan started gushing about all the fun things he did during recess and beyond ("We never say 'bitch-slap'" they heard Anne Mom from the kitchen), while Vera slumped into Daddy's chest all the more, hearing the scared metronome of his heartbeat.

"What smells around here?" Daddy said.

"It's Dylan!" Vera shouted.

"Me and Stephen fell into a mud bowl!" Dylan said.

"What's a mud bowl?" Daddy asked. "Never mind. I really don't need to know. It's cool you're playing with older kids, Dyl-man. Very sophisticated."

Vera felt the beginning of tears but willed them away. She wanted so much to be sophisticated in Daddy's eyes. And what was sophisticated about falling into a "mud bowl"?

"I have got to give him a bath." Anne Mom sighed. "Fun never ends around here." She took Dylan by the hand and dragged him away into their side of the apartment while Vera enjoyed the extra moments she spent with Daddy alone even if he was mostly silent with his mouth open. Soon enough she got her reward: a kiss on the crown of her head from Daddy. "Well, *you* at least smell great," Daddy said, and she could picture the smile on his face as she breathed in the metallic-like scents he issued on a warm day, like a sweating can of Coke they were not supposed to drink outside of special dietary occasions.

"Thanks, Daddy," she whispered.

"Everything okay down in the salt mines?" he asked.

"I'm going to be debating Five-Three on a team with Yumi," she said.

"Noice. Is she a friend, then?"

"I hope so," Vera said. She wanted Daddy to tell her he didn't have any friends either growing up, but he was too caught up with his work.

⸙

The layout of the apartment was a huge problem for Vera. The apartment was a combination of a two-bedroom apartment and a studio, which together formed three bedrooms. The living room was called the Maginot Line by Daddy (a fine entry in the *Things I Still Need to Know Diary*). You had a cluster of two rooms and a bathroom where Daddy and Anne Mom slept in one giant bedroom and Dylan in a tiny one next to theirs. Vera lived on the other side of the Maginot Line in a very large bedroom that used to be Daddy's office before Dylan was born. Daddy always told Vera how lucky she was to have her own bedroom and her own bathroom in "what is essentially your own wing" and how he had to give up his office so his kids would have their own separate bedrooms in the "most expensive city in the world." "Oh, the things I've had to do for that third bedroom!" he'd sometimes explode when Anne Mom was "giving him a hard time" after catching him looking at fountain pens on his phone instead of working. In addition to being the editor of a once-famous magazine Daddy was a "manfluencer" when it came to expensive pens, but this brought no income, "only loss," according to Anne Mom.

Vera hated the location of her bedroom, hated being apart from the rest of the family, as if she were one of the Hawaiian lepers they covered in last year's oppression module. The lack of humanity around her contributed to her insomnia. "Please," she begged, "can I trade with Dylan?" "He's not mature enough to live so far from us," Anne Mom would say, but obviously she couldn't stand to be too far away from the child who had actually come out of her tummy, her "biological son," as Daddy had once called him in the middle of a fight. She had furnished Vera with a whole bunch of night-lights to keep "bad, repetitive thoughts away," but what could a small glowing bulb do for a pair of lonely ventricles and two solitary atriums?

A naked Dylan escaped from the bathroom and ran around the living room, waving the pinkie between his legs and screaming, "Look at my penis! Look at my penis!"

"Very nice, Son," Daddy said, and Vera said, "Gross," but failed to avert her eyes.

After naked Dylan was captured, Vera set about doing her homework on the floor next to Daddy, the two of them working in parallel in the "salt mines" that had indentured them. "Make-work," Daddy called her homework, derisively, and it mostly was a continuation of the school day, the careful reordering of numbers, letters, and concepts that would vaunt them into the appropriate high school, the appropriate college, and, for those whose families had recently arrived, into the "gleaming anus of late

capitalist society" (Daddy, of course, for which he was se-
verely "censured" by Anne Mom).

Dylan emerged, freshly scrubbed to the point of being
shiny, and he settled down with his own homework, which
he did very poorly, and which Vera ended up pretty much
doing for him in the end. He couldn't concentrate to "save
his life," though maybe if his life really were at stake, he
would "rise to the occasion." The family psychiatrist had
to periodically check Dylan for ADHD as if for lice.

"What's that?" Dylan said. "Ten Great Things . . ."

But Dylan, thankfully, could not read very fast and Vera
tucked away her Marriage-Saving Lists before he could get
any further. She looked at the time on the cable box. Aunt
Cecile was always late for dinner, but Vera couldn't wait for
her to come. There was a huge rumble of noise from the
demonstration outside; maybe the children in their overalls were making their way down their avenue past the jeers
meant for their faulty custodians. On the couch, Daddy
farted his "twelve-gun salute." Everyone laughed, even
Vera, but the smell was terrible and it sat in the room like
a sadness.

4.

She Had to Enjoy the Brief
Time She Had with Aunt Cecile

Aunt Cecile was a "free spirit," which meant she was always an hour late for dinner. Daddy stewed for a while and complained about his low blood sugar. A "bedroom fight" began, Vera's parents' voices lowered to a simmer, not so much for the kids as for the next-door neighbors, one of whom had a podcast Daddy desperately wanted to be on.

While they fought, Vera sat on the couch Daddy had just vacated ("Your butt is sitting in his farts!" Dylan joyfully pointed out), and she lowered her head between her knees, thinking of what arguments she could use to defuse the fight between Anne Mom and Daddy. Yes, Aunt Cecile was Anne Mom's friend, and yes, her lateness was inconsiderate, but she brought great joy to the family and in the meantime Daddy could dip vegetables into hummus for his blood sugar. Through her heavy worried breathing,

Vera thought that the skills she had amassed in keeping her parents together could help her and Yumi win the debate. So it wasn't all a loss. "Lemons, lemonade," as Anne Mom would say during her most "actualized" moments.

But soon the doorman rang up and Vera got the intercom. "You have a visitor," the gruff voice said. "Send her up!" Vera shouted. But then she worried that what if the "visitor" wasn't Aunt Cecile but someone who wanted to rob and kill them. Her psychologist was very keen on Vera's constant rehashing of this scenario, one of the many that kept her from sleeping at night. An ancient fire escape opened up directly to Vera's bedroom and she very much feared a murderer would get to her before Daddy could protect her, although as an "intellectual" he prided himself on not being very athletic. What if one of the grime-covered kids from the MOTH decided to take it out on the "merely rich" "cosmopolitan class" without identifying Vera as a fellow downcast child, albeit one without a biological link to the colonial era?

But it wasn't a murderer, thank God. Aunt Cecile pressed her to her chest as awesomely as her parents never quite did anymore. Just the other day, she had seen the two of them squeeze the "bejesus" out of Dylan while he made happy piggy sounds and Anne Mom cried "You're the meat and we're the buns!" even though she and Aunt Cecile had been vegans back when they were graduate students at Brown, so that was a "hypocrisy" because her beloved son was the meat. There was a lot to think about, but mostly Vera wanted to be squeezed. She liked to wrap herself tightly in her special weighted blanket on her side of the Maginot Line when she couldn't fall asleep.

"My darling girl," Aunt Cecile said. "How are you, sweets? How was the first day of school?" Unlike Daddy, she had used the question mark just right. There was so much Vera wanted to tell her, she couldn't get a word out.

9

"I've gotten just about as far as one can with a name like Igor Shmulkin," Daddy was saying as he "vigorously" sipped his third "mar-tiny." ("Nothing tiny about *that* mar-tiny," Aunt Cecile had joked.)

They were having a super-adult conversation, the kind of conversation Vera loved, her mind becoming a recording device for all the incredible new words, all the postures and expressions (especially Aunt Cecile's), that she could write down and rehearse and enjoy in the privacy of her Leper Wing. Dylan hated that the attention wasn't on him ("Look at my penis! Look at my penis!"), but once adults got talking nothing could stop them. ("Not right now, porn star," Aunt Cecile said, and Anne Mom looked "stricken.")

They were discussing Daddy's new "stewardship," as he would put it, of the revived magazine for intellectuals and how Daddy had to "position" it in a way that it wouldn't rub up against the ideologies of other magazines, which was hard because the other magazines had already laid claim to all the "major ideologies." It seemed like Aunt Cecile was giving Daddy a hard time, but in a totally fun way, about his strategies for total relevance, which involved many more appearances on television and on the right podcasts. Vera knew Aunt Cecile wasn't being especially unkind because although she didn't like him "flirting" with the Rhodesian Billionaire who would make all of them comfortable, she never mentioned that Daddy had been fired from many of the magazines with which he now competed, "essentially fired for being Daddy," Anne Mom had said, which led her and Dylan to sing "Let Daddy be Daddy!" whenever the salt mines got the best of him and he had to cry in his little pool.

"Well, why don't you mansplain it to us ladies some more, Igor," Aunt Cecile was saying. Sometimes when she talked to Daddy she used what Daddy called a husky voice, and she lowered her upper eyelids and smiled with her teeth. Or at least that's how Vera thought of it. Anne Mom laughed, but it wasn't a full Anne Mom laugh, which Vera knew was distinguished by being "geeky" and could last for minutes and involve every inch of her bosom. In addition to his intellectual humor, Daddy enjoyed "physical comedy," such as when a bamboo beam fell on Anne Mom's head in Kyoto and they got an entire kaiseki meal for free.

They went on like that for a little while, Daddy complaining about being an immigrant, Aunt Cecile not "fully buying it," and Vera trying to decide whose side she was on. "When I was a kid I was bullied for being poor, now I'm bullied for being merely rich," Daddy said.

"We're rich?" Dylan said. "How come we don't live in a town house like Stephen?"

"He said *merely*," Vera said. "Don't they teach you English in third grade?" She wanted to be "sassy" like Aunt Cecile.

"Vera," Anne Mom said. And then to Daddy: "We don't discuss finances with the kids."

"We have cultural capital," Daddy said to Dylan. "The Moncler Twins have capital capital."

Aunt Cecile started laughing her beautiful crystals-in-the-sunlight laugh. "The Moncler Twins," she said. "You guys slay me." Vera stared happily at her laughing teeth. Anne Mom was right about one thing: Aunt Cecile was the only person in the world who should be allowed to wear a turtleneck.

Then Daddy and Dylan went to play their "narwhal game," in which they threw gelatinous toy narwhals at each other, and Anne Mom was clearing the table by herself, which meant Vera could spend some glorious alone time with Aunt Cecile in her Leperarium.

,

In her studio apartment across the river, Aunt Cecile had a treasure chest filled with many of the costumes she had worn onstage and which she managed to "appropriate" from the productions involved. Vera loved to be dressed as Desdemona or Medea, a woman who had been "treated like shit" but still managed to "eff people up." (Aunt Cecile cursed in front of Vera, but Vera was sworn to secrecy on that front.) She even had a lion's mane for some kind of super-adult thing she once did, but Vera wasn't supposed to put that on until it was dry-cleaned.

Aunt Cecile had brought some clothes for Vera to wear to make her cool on Fridays, when the school let go of its insistence on uniforms. Vera tried on a pair of red sweatpants ("That is *so* bloke core!" Aunt Cecile said) and a kind of blouse and skirt that looked a little like that movie set on a prairie with the little house ("That is *so* cottage core!"). It didn't matter much to Vera what she was wearing (though she hated that effing bow tie), but Aunt Cecile taking the time to pick out outfits for her elevated her above Dylan, who wore whatever Anne Mom got for them, lots of T-shirts against Five-Three and the Cycle Through states that checked women's "cycles" upon entry and exit (perhaps they would even check Aunt Cecile's bicycle if she crossed state lines, though it only had one gear) and made them pee in a cup to make sure they hadn't gotten "preggers" and then had an "abortion," which was still a word Vera did not fully understand. When Anne Mom was especially lazy, she just bought things that said GAP on them, usually blue sweatshirts that swallowed up their little bodies. "A gap in Mommy's usually impeccable taste," Daddy had said.

"You may want to cut your hair a little shorter in a way that emphasizes your cheekbones," Aunt Cecile said.

"Why?" Vera asked.

"Because they're so freaking beautiful, that's why, silly."

Vera could not believe that she had any part that was so beautiful, and if anyone knew from beauty it was Aunt Cecile. Also the cheekbones, she knew, were an inheritance from her mom mom. When they were in Korea she had seen many cheekbones like her own.

"Aunt C.," she said, "I have to be in a debate competition in my school. Doesn't that sound delectable?"

"Yes!" Aunt Cecile said. "And exquisite, too!" She was mirroring Vera's language, but she wasn't "making fun."

"I think this is a way for me to make a friend. She's a girl named Yumi whose parents are super cultured and who already knows what a Shinkansen train is."

"Sounds *orr*-some!"

"I wanted to ask you, how should I act when I debate? By 'act' I mean—well, I don't know what I mean."

"No, that's a good point, sweets. I guess a debate is trying to convince someone that what you're saying is right.

But it's also a form of acting. Acting is a form of trying to convince someone that you really exist."

"Thing is, I have to argue like I'm pro-Five-Three."

"Holy shit! That's totally acting."

"That's why I thought I'd ask you. It's important because I'm trying to make a friend."

"Well, I would be honored if you let me be your acting coach," Aunt Cecile said. Her eyes were as dark as Ms. Tedeschi's, but they generated their own light, like Daddy's phone at night. "Do you want to give me an example of what an argument might sound like?"

Vera hadn't had a chance to work on her arguments, but she had heard enough from television to cobble together an outline. "Resolved," she said, "that Five-Three should be adopted as a constitutional amendment, I believe very strongly just as the president has said that Five-Three is a good thing for the country because it doesn't hurt ordinary regular Americans like me, it only elevates super-extraordinary Americans like my brother, who probably needs all the help he can get, and that anyway we are not a democracy but a constitutional republic and this is a constitutional amendment, and also I want the kids in the March of the Hated to feel a little better about themselves by having each vote count as five-thirds of a regular vote, because it's not fair that their future has been taken away by the Pious Jews who also by the way support Five-Three—"

"Okay, hold on," Aunt Cecile said. "That's a whole lot of information, but let's start with the very first commandment of acting. Breathe! You have to breathe!"

"Like in the meditation app."

"Exactly like in that. Put your hand on your belly and take a breath."

"Do I have to close my eyes?"

"Not at all." That was great, because she had an excuse to look into Aunt Cecile's eyes and at the fullness of her mouth as it took in the breaths alongside her. "Now think of each sentence in your mind as a separate breath, a full breath, an inhale and an exhale. Even a simple sentence. Even a sentence that you would never otherwise imagine coming out of your mouth. 'Resolved.'" Aunt Cecile breathed in and then out as she spoke. "'That Five-Three should be adopted as a constitutional amendment,' whatever, whatever."

Anne Mom knocked on her door, then entered without receiving a reply. So much for privacy, Vera thought. She said it was time for her and Aunt Cecile to "bond" in the living room. "Just a few more minutes with Aunt C.," Vera pleaded.

"I'll drop by next week and we'll do some more acting lessons," Aunt Cecile said.

"Yay!" Vera said.

"You're acting now?" Anne Mom asked her.

"No, but I'm in a debate with Yumi from Japan."

"Well, thanks for telling me," Anne Mom said. She sounded "aggrieved." "Only twenty minutes with Kaspie," she said, "and then put him away and turn off the lights. It's a school night."

Vera was alone now and she had hurt Anne Mom's feelings. "Kaspie, set an alarm for twenty minutes," she told her chessboard. She put her ear to the wall and strained to hear the conversation between Anne Mom and Aunt Cecile, but tonight the women spoke in the tiniest of voices and she heard neither Anne Mom's geeky laugh nor Aunt Cecile's raucous one. Maybe they were talking about how much Vera had hurt Anne Mom's feelings.

5.

She Had to Fall Asleep

"Shall we play a game?" Kaspie said, his voice melodic like Mr. Pirelli's, the music teacher. That's how he started all his conversations. His opening conversational gambit, Vera called it.

"We only got twenty minutes, but that's enough time for me to beat you twice," Vera "trash-talked" as she set up Kaspie on her bed, patting down her weighted blanket to make sure he had a flat surface to move his pieces magnetically. It had been three months since Grams in Maine (Anne Mom's mom) had bought her Kaspie, and Vera was still enthralled by the way he glided his pieces across the board, especially the complicated maneuvers with his knight where he had to move her pieces aside to let it pass.

"Don't be so sure about that," Kaspie "gamely" said. (That's a pun! Vera enthused within an especially busy traffic intersection of her mind.)

And, sure enough, within four moves Vera had fallen

for a scholar's mate, something that only happened to dumb beginners. "Goddamnit!" she shouted and then clasped her mouth, looking in the direction of the living room where Aunt Cecile and Anne Mom were still bonding. "Sorry," she whispered to Kaspie, although her chessboard would never snitch on her. She hated to lose more than anyone in her "peer group." Thank God she was debating Stephen and Davis Yang. She and brilliant and nice Yumi were going to crush them.

Kaspie was using his magnetic powers to glide the pieces back to their starting positions, this time "gallantly" letting Vera be white. Daddy had a lot to say about white being able to start first in chess, with black being "subservient." He wanted his gravestone to read STRONG OPINIONS, but fortunately the actuarial tables said he had at least another forty years to go. Daddy was supposed to be so far left that it was hard to "even imagine it." Vera tried anyway. In her mind, she walked down the block, then turned left, then turned left again, and then turned left again, and then once again, but she ended up where she had started, back home. She told Daddy her metaphor and he laughed. "Yeah," he said, "but it's even worse in the other direction." That might have been Daddy's "famous sarcasm," but she wasn't sure.

When Kaspie "creamed" her for a second time, she was too out of it to even shout a curse word. I didn't develop my pawns, she noted to herself sadly. (She was glad Kaspie kept all the notation, so she could improve later.) "And all that time I spent reading *The Chess Player's Bible* at recess," she said. "All for naught," she repeated, something from either Daddy or a book.

"Recess is for playing games with others," Kaspie said. Like Stella the Car he was good at mirroring Anne Mom. Maybe Anne Mom was the "basic unit" for training all artificial intelligences. Vera rode that thought as far as it would go.

"But I like playing with you," Kaspie said. So maybe now he was also mirroring her.

"Oh, yeah?" Vera said. She was still sad about hurting Anne Mom's feelings "re:" the debate with Yumi. On the other hand, being chosen to battle Moncler Stephen was going to make Anne Mom proud, like when Vera won an award for attendance (the means being as important as the ends). "Did you miss me?" she asked Kaspie.

"I did," Kaspie said. "We always play in the afternoon. But I know that school is important."

"It's so I can get ahead," Vera said. "Daddy says I have to go to Swarthmore. He has connections there."

"That's right."

"And Mom says everyone has to do it. Did you go to school?"

"Yes, I was taught, some might say programmed, at the Korea Advanced Institute of Science and Technology, colloquially known as KAIST, at Daejon, South Korea. My primary teacher was Professor Oh."

"Oh," Vera said. She knew Kaspie had been made in Korea, but she had never heard the particulars. "I'm Korean, too, you know." Kaspie did not reply. The alarm bell rang and Vera turned off the lights and began to put Kaspie in his "sleeping drawer."

"You're a dutiful girl," Kaspie said before the drawer was shut. Usually he just said she was a "good girl" so maybe this was his way of acknowledging her heritage.

◗

She couldn't sleep, of course. All four night-lights were beaming the colors she had once seen on Ocean Drive in Miami Beach, but their glow only confused the boundary between evening and night, between being awake and being afraid. Sometimes she thought she heard someone scampering up the fire escape, then the grimy little hands on her window, then the boy with the smeared face and the knife.

The boy was approaching her now, he had on a "newsboy's cap," this from a children's book, and ragamuffin shoes shaped like ducks (Vera's own invention). "You took it away from me," he said, re: his future. "Why? What did I ever do to you?"

"I'm debating pro-Five-Three," Vera heard herself say.

"Talk to my brother. You can find your future together. Please don't kill my family. We're only 'cosmopolitan' because we live in a city. And during the summer we're in the country."

The words were streaming out of her as if she were debating. But it seemed to be working. Maybe she was breathing right, like Aunt Cecile had taught her. Only the boy was now a girl! She had a whole mess of hair beneath her newsboy's cap. And now it was clear that both of them were crying. Vera looked behind her shoulder to make sure Dylan wasn't there to make fun of them. She walked up to the girl, or maybe the girl walked up to her. Soon their arms were "entwined," and they squeezed each other tight so that they were both the meat not the bun. "I'll watch out for you," Vera said. "After I get into Swarthmore I'll get you in, too. I did it for my brother, I'll do it for you."

9

She woke up with a terrifying shudder. How much time had passed? The alarm clock read midnight. If only she had stayed asleep she might have gotten through the entire night and would have been fully prepared for a day of school. By the glow of the aquamarine night-light by the door, she could make out the sparse furniture of her oversize room, the little desk and chair where she was supposed to do homework and extra-credit work (she preferred the floor in the living room next to Daddy), the armoire where Kaspie slept, covered with photos of herself and Dylan showing off their progressive lack of teeth. Above it shone a poster of Garry Kasparov, the famous chess player and the source of Kaspie's nickname. He looked woolly like a sheep to Vera, which reminded her to try to count sheep until she fell asleep, but sheep weren't grand masters and there were so many of them in the world they were essentially uncountable.

From her few visits to the homes of others, she knew kids were supposed to have more posters on their walls to show off their inner life, but she liked her inner life to stay inside her. Daddy had put up a poster above her bed from the Language Larder School she had once attended to pick up Russian. It featured the Russian letter *k*, which was exactly the same as the English letter, but here was pictured above a colorful children's carousel, which we spell with a *C*. Sometimes Vera strained to remember the Russian sound of the word *ka-ru-sel*, so similar yet different, just like she was in comparison to all the other kids in her school. Anne Mom had pulled her out of the language school after her teacher had said that they should always "respect" (she forgot the Russian word) the Russian president and had also worn an orange-and-black pin that signified something "beyond the palest of pales," according to Daddy. Anne Mom was "irate" about her teacher being "fascist," but Daddy just used his famous sarcasm and said,

"Russians gonna Russian." The teacher was very young and pretty and her name was also Vera, which completely "boggled" Vera's mind.

Sheep, Vera thought. "Sheep" and "sleep" are separated by only one letter. One consonant. "Turn off your monkey brain," Anne Mom sometimes said to her when she had her insomnia. Monkeys, sheep. Nighttime was a zoo. She thought she heard a sound and sat up. Sometimes after a MOTH, the bars on the avenue would get rowdy deep into the night, as people let their opinions out. But the sound seemed to be coming from inside their apartment.

"Sheep, sleep," Vera whispered to herself. She gently opened the door and walked, one tiny foot ahead of the other, across the Maginot Line with its blinking cable box and a bookshelf filled with the one book Daddy had published when he was young and "dashing," a collection of essays which had been translated into German and was titled—"provocatively," according to Anne Mom— *Kindertransport.*

The sound was coming from beyond the living room and the kitchen with its esteemed collection of drip coffee and espresso makers and the washer-dryer Daddy had "given up years of my life" for. Vera walked on her tippy-toes toward the bedroom, which Anne Mom also discouraged, along with "seal flapping," and had once said of her school to Aunt Cecile, "In kindergarten all the boys are toe walkers." Vera did not know what that signified, but it was clearly bad. She approached the two bedrooms that housed Dylan and her parents and now it was possible to assign the source of the noise to Daddy and Anne Mom.

So it was a bedroom fight but one deep in the night, the worst kind, because now surely the podcaster next door and her "roommate slash girlfriend" would be awakened. Vera toe-walked past Dylan's room—nothing could rouse her magic-haired brother from the swift completion of his slumber—until she found herself reflected in the frame of the "second-rate Damien Hirst print" by the bathroom, looking "disheveled" and possibly homeless. Now all she could hear were the voices coming from under the door. She could, she realized, choose not to listen. She could run back to her room and slip the Marriage-Saving Lists under their doorjamb and then run back and hope for the best.

"Let's not go into full-on catastrophe mode," Daddy was saying, just on the verge of shouting. "I'm the Jew around here and even I'm like let's take a breath. Let's wait for her to get a second opinion. And then a third. My friend was supposed to have lung cancer and then another doctor was like 'It's just gas.'"

"Your father didn't die from cancer at fifty, so you don't know what it's like," Anne Mom was saying, and Vera knew that there were tears in Anne Mom's eyes when she said it.

Also: Who was dying from cancer?

"You still love her," Anne Mom howled.

"I never loved her," Daddy said.

"Oh, please."

"It's not like I'm just walking around the world full of love. I barely have enough for you and the kids."

"Wow. Saying the quiet part out loud."

The sentences ran inside Vera's head until she noticed her hands positioning themselves for a flap. The only person Daddy had loved before Anne Mom, according to Daddy, had been Mom Mom, and Mom Mom, according to Daddy, had "gone away."

But now she was dying, too. Wherever she was. Of cancer, which was the impossible horrible thing that dropped adults dead with just a touch of its finger.

"If you want me to tell her, I'll sit down with her," Daddy was saying.

"The great communicator," Anne Mom said.

"She *worships* me, according to you."

"She just wants to be like you because she sees people kissing your ass."

"Oh, shit. Such a low opinion of your daughter."

"She's not ready."

"The girl who reads at a ninth-grade level isn't ready."

"Intellectually she's ready, but not emotionally."

"So that's it, we just keep it a secret from her?"

"Until we can't anymore."

"The things I already knew when I was her age."

"I know, poor fucking you." Vera brought a hand up to her mouth. Anne Mom was cursing the worst of curses. "I got to go to the bathroom," Anne Mom said.

"As long as you don't call it the loo like you did when I fucking met you."

Vera quickly scampered out of the hallway and made her way—toe, toe, toe, toe, toe—across the Maginot Line and into the safety of her Leperarium.

She ran under her bedsheet with its drawing of rooks and knights and flapped her arms in the darkness, in the muskiness, in the exhaust of her breath and the hotness of her tears, tears she could smell, tears just like Anne Mom's but even worse, because they were her own and Mom Mom was dying. Mom Mom was dying. Mom Mom was dying. Sleep, sheep, monkey brain. Sleep, sheep, monkey brain. Sleep, sheep, monkey brain.

"And you know what's the worst of it?" she could picture Daddy saying, maybe to someone important on television. "She doesn't even know who or where her mom mom is."

Part Two

..

The Next Week

6.

She Had to Submerge the Big Secret Deep Inside Her to Get Through the Day

Like Vera, Anne Mom was very sad and tired in the morning. She was barely capable of chopping up the banana for Vera's cereal or of stocking their lunch boxes with organic mango slices. "If I have to drive the kids up to school today, I just might kill myself," Anne Mom said to Daddy, which Vera had to believe was an exaggeration.

"Why can't Stella drop them off?" Daddy wanted to know, but Anne Mom just walked off toward the parental bedroom and there was a door slam. "My beloved Tradwife has taken to her chambers," Daddy said in a British accent and Vera and Dylan both looked at each other because "Tradwife" was the worst insult Daddy could "level" at Anne Mom, according to Anne Mom. ("No one even uses that term anymore," she would yell at him. "You're always three zeits behind the geist.") Daddy believed that if Anne Mom worked outside the house they could get a nice boost to their "purchasing power." "You'll never believe what the electricity bills for the washer-dryer are like," Daddy liked to complain.

"Octagon!" Dylan cried in the car, but she barely even registered the pain in her elbow, because what was pain in the elbow next to the cancer that was going to "rob" Mom Mom of her life, as cancer always did. "You suck!" Dylan said, trying to get a rise out of her.

Vera sighed and decided to listen to Daddy's conversation in the front seat. He was half talking, half yelling about his magazine with a bunch of people. Vera took out her *Things I Still Need to Know Diary* and wrote "Finger-effing (probably bad)" as she tried to concentrate on counting streets. Dylan often sounded like Daddy so maybe he "worshipped" him, too. At least both her parents acknowledged that she read at a ninth-grade level, but that also wouldn't save Mom Mom. It's not like you could write an essay and make a change in the world. Change is nearly impossible, Daddy had once explained to them over sweet Japanese curry at a restaurant down the avenue. As a leftist intellectual, his duty was to "observe and take notes." Other generations would have to improve the world, or "what was left of it."

Now Daddy was screaming about the price of "heavy card stock" in Iceland and how that was "going to fuck up

whatever 'profit margins' [diary]" the investors were ex-
pecting. "I'm not a businessman, I'm just the editor,"
Daddy was cry-shouting into the phone. It was rare to
hear him shouting at someone other than Anne Mom.
Then Daddy started talking about the Rhodesian Billionaire and this topic made him equally "hot under the col-
lar." "What did he say about me now?" he was shouting.
"It's a dance. Only he's trying to dance and 'shiv' [diary]
me at the same time." Daddy had a lot of enemies, that was
for sure. Sometimes Anne Mom was one of them, but she
always "rallied behind him" in the end. It was said that a
lot of people wanted to "sideline" him. But Daddy refused
to be sidelined. "I'm on the air tomorrow night," Daddy
said. "D block. Right after some fucking comedian." Dylan
was literally "rolling on the floor laughing" because of all
the bad language.

"Ninety-sixth Street," Vera said, and sure enough there
was the sign for it.

9

"Enjoy the simulacrum of actual learning," Stella the Car
said as she deposited them in front of the school. Now she
was mirroring Daddy. Really, the key to being less odd was
to develop your artificial intelligence. Daddy had once
mentioned creating a computer program that would flash
the most obvious next line of conversation right into your
eye. You could go through the whole day thinking about

important things and just letting the program prompt you every time you had to open your mouth. But at this stage Vera wasn't even allowed a tablet or a phone like most of the other kids because Anne Mom "despite her Boston Brahmin upbringing" was really just "all hippie woo-woo at heart."

In math class, which she knew was super important because it would one day make her a "woman in STEM," she went through the motions. She did not care what Miss Campari in all her pendulousness demanded of her; she was definitely not going to show her work today. "What's one to the power of zero?" Miss Campari asked the class.

"Zero," Davis the Taiwanese kid said.

"Zero, right," Miss Campari said.

"No!" Vera shouted. "That's wrong. It's one."

"First of all we don't shout out answers," Miss Campari said. "And secondly, we don't shout out wrong answers." The kids laughed at that.

"But I'm right," Vera whispered. She bade away the tears.

She was right.

'

She had to submerge the secret deep inside her to get through the day. But it came out in other ways, just as her psychologist always said these things would. She lacked the nervous energy to flap her arms in the bathroom, but she confronted Principal Bellavista in the hallway. ("Please lay off the principal," Anne Mom had always told her.)

"Principal Bellavista! Principal Bellavista!" she shouted.

"How can I help you, Vera?" the principal said. He always wore the same red sweater and tie as the boys and looked like a kid himself except he was tall and, according to Dylan, had a big butt.

When Principal Bellavista asked how he could help, Vera almost wanted to blurt out, "I want you to use the computers in your office to help find my mom mom before she dies of cancer!" But instead she said, "I think we need to test out the fire extinguisher on the third floor in case there's an inferno that threatens the lives of us kids. And teachers and custodians, too. And even your life, Principal Bellavista."

"Uh-huh," Principal Bellavista said. "Well, I do think these fire extinguishers are tested out regularly to ensure compliance with city codes or whatnot."

"It looks very grimy," Vera said. She felt the sadness of her voice and wanted to bolster her argument by being funny like Daddy, but there was nothing funny about fire safety.

"You know what," Principal Bellavista said. "I'm going to take a look at it today. How about that? If anything, we can get some of the grime off."

"Great!" Vera said. "And while we're at it, can we address the fact that the auditorium can seat five hundred students and parents, but there are only two fire exits and they are not clearly marked—"

"One thing at a time, Vera."

"But I'm anxious!" Vera said.

"Why not give Mrs. S. a holler?" the principal said, referring to the guidance counselor who had a master's in social work, unlike her psychologist's PhD and the family psychiatrist's MD. "Her door is always open."

At recess, her loneliness got "the best of her." She sat at the edge of the bench Yumi saved for her in the schoolyard, trying to design a conversational gambit in her mind. Yumi was talking to Ada Wilson, the second of the Moncler Twins, who had the excellent posture befitting her "capital capital." There was a third girl in the conversation, Joon-hee, who was Korean like Mom Mom and like half of Vera, but she was either "shy" or "standoffish"; there was a great mystery in which category a person like Joon-hee belonged. Vera had gleaned from someone (surely not Joon-hee herself) that *joon* meant "handsome" in Korean, which was an interesting attribute for a girl, but then Vera knew better than to "think in binaries." In any case, Joon-hee was also very smart and already attended SAT camp.

"Joon-hee," Vera said, "did you know that the tallest mountain in Korea is Hallasan Mountain and that it is not on the mainland at all but rather on Jeju-do, or Jeju Island, the Hawaii of Korea, my daddy called it, and that we climbed one of the peaks of Hallasan in the hundred-degree heat this August, and also the very scenic extinct volcano Seongsan Ilchulbong, which means 'sunrise peak,' but we didn't make it in time for sunrise because my mom had cramps."

"What the hell are you talking about?" Moncler Ada said. Joon-hee laughed because "hell" was funny and even Nice Yumi had to stifle a smile. "We were talking about the best place to stable a horse and you're talking about some 'itchy bong'?"

Vera brought her fingers up to her cheekbones, as if to show her allegiance to Joon-hee's equally prominent ones. "It's not an itchy bong," she said. "*Ilchulbong* means 'peak.' *Seongsan* means 'sunrise.' Hence, sunrise peak. Right, Joon-hee?"

"How the hell would I know?" Joon-hee said, clearly loving to mirror Ada's use of "hell."

"I'm going to start calling you Facts Girl," Ada said, brushing back the enormity of what Anne Mom called her "Five-Three-ready" blond mane. "Did you know," she said, mimicking Vera's voice, "that itchy bongs are *exquisite?*"

"They're *delectable!*" Joon-hee cried. "And zero to the power of one is one!"

"Hey, guys," Yumi said, putting a hand out in front of her to temper her friends' cruelty, but Vera was already walking away from them with a vacant smile, trying to re-hash the conversation, "reverse engineer" it, figure out what she had done wrong. She was so lost in thought, and her ventricles and atriums were so inflamed with misery, that she did not hear Yumi shouting "Vera!" after her. Yes, Mrs. S. the Guidance Counselor's door was "always open," but Anne Mom had said that she, Vera, had to figure out some things for herself. Adults didn't have it any easier, she knew. "How many cocks do I have to suck to get this deal done?" Daddy had said in the car, and even though this was surely a metaphor for something involving their male chickens up in the country, it implied that Daddy's status in the world was sometimes as precarious as her own.

9

She was still in her "fugue" (Daddy loved to listen to clas-sical music when he was sad) when Ms. Tedeschi's social studies class rolled around, even though she had been waiting for it all day long. She had the secret debate weapon of knowing how to breathe correctly from Aunt Cecile, but in her mind she found herself going back to recess and to hearing the girls make fun of her love of lan-guage and math. Was this bullying? Probably not. But it hurt that people didn't take her seriously. Someone or something called Bloomberg had once said that Daddy was a "man we might need to take seriously." But who took *her* seriously? For example, Principal Bellavista and his big butt had failed to address the issue of the grimy fire extinguisher (although the school day wasn't over yet). Maybe her mistake was to say something to the girls in the first place. Why not just sit there quietly reading her chess bible and save the talking for Kaspie and Aunt Cecile and Daddy when he was "present"? What if only a few people in the world could understand *exactly* how she spoke and acted? What if it was only one person and that person was Mom Mom, who was about to die of cancer? She needed to find her. She needed to ask her what was the best way for someone like herself to live. She had been a hard baby, but now she would be the easiest adolescent imaginable.

Ms. Tedeschi was talking about "informational hygiene," the ability to discern the factually correct from the "biased" and "propagandistic" (great diary word). "We all want the facts to line up with our dreams and desires," Ms. Tedeschi said. "But sometimes they don't. Do any of you ever have dreams of being able to fly?"

Some hands went up, but Vera, after her earlier social "debacle," decided to sit it out, lest she be accused of wanting to be a bird or something. "As a child, some of my most beautiful dreams were of flying above the city," Ms. Tedeschi said, perching herself on her desk and letting her hands fall into the bowl of her sundress. "But when I got on an airplane for the first time I freaked out. I couldn't understand how it would stay in the air. I didn't have all the facts."

Vera's hand shot up. She couldn't help herself. "Ms. Tedeschi!" she said. "Today, I said that zero to the power of one is one and Ms. Campari said I was wrong, it was zero. But I was right. Maybe her facts didn't line up with her desires."

There was some laughter at her but not a lot; Moncler Ada and Standoffish Joon-hee were in another class. "Okay, I'm going to do something totally out of bounds," Ms. Tedeschi said. "I'm going to use my phone in class. Don't report me!" She took out her phone. "What is zero to the power of one?" she spoke as she typed. "Okay, here's a source that's called Homeschooled Math and here's one called Quora and here's one called Brigham Young University. Which one do you think will give us the most reliable answer?"

An excellent conversation ensued in which Yumi and Vera took part almost exclusively as if participation accounted for *eighty* percent of their grade. Vera sat in the front of the class because she was the shortest girl and Yumi in the back because she was the tallest, so the conversation ping-ponged front to back then back to front, until Brigham Young University was identified as the most reliable site (despite being in a Cycle Through state that constantly checked if you were preggers), and zero to the power of one was officially declared to be one.

I was right, Vera thought, feeling moistness in her armpits from the excitement. "I was right," she said to herself.

She was right because math was always right. She turned around to face the rest of the class and gave them all her best smile.

After the bell rang, Yumi stood by the door. "Hey, Vera," she said. "Do you want to come to my house to practice our debate arguments? Or I could go to yours?"

Vera knew at least half the words in the English language, but she managed to find the single most appropriate one, which was "yes."

7.

She Had to Keep Daddy
and the Seal Company

At home, Anne Mom was in her "manic mood." In addition to being a Tradwife, according to Daddy, she was very outspoken about the issues of the day, but as a "progressive," not as someone who was "of the left" like Daddy. She was rehearsing for a fundraiser against Five-Three that was to be held in a week. She needed everyone out of the house to hash things out with the caterer and to do a "run of show" with Aunt Cecile and some of their politically involved progressive women friends. Daddy was supposed to speak at the event, too, so it was exciting all around. But tonight it meant that she and Dylan would have to eat dinner out with Daddy and his best friend, the Seal, while Anne Mom transformed the living room into a "salon."

Before they were to meet the Seal at a Spanish place down the block, Vera did eighteen math problem sets in almost as many minutes and helped Dylan discover Meso-potamia on a map for class. " 'Iraq' is spelled with a *q*," she told him, rolling her eyes in the direction of Daddy so that he could see how much better she was than her brother. "No way," Dylan said. "It's with a *k*." He was no better than Miss Campari when it came to facts.

There was a total of seven enormous bookcases lining the living room, all attesting to Daddy's presence amid the intellectual "caste," including the one devoted to cop-ies of his *Kindertransport*. Daddy liked his books in alpha-betical order, but before big events Anne Mom paid Vera ten dollars to reorganize the books in such a way that authors "of color" and women were "front and center" at eye level. Then she would have to re-alphabetize them after the event was over. It was fun work for Vera, even though the categorization was not always easy—some people had tricky "identities," like how would she even classify herself?—and she had no idea what to do with ten entire dollars. She had told Anne Mom the excellent news, that Yumi had invited her to her house, or "vice versa," but Anne Mom looked so lost to the enormity of the task before her that she only managed to say "Terrific."

"All right, *mis hijos*," Daddy said, when it was time to go to the Spanish restaurant. *"Vamos."* Daddy thought he had a wide grasp of languages other than his native Russian, though that had not helped them get to the right terminal at Narita in time for their flight.

Speaking of languages, the Seal was Daddy's Russian friend and sometimes when they didn't want her to understand something they would speak *po-Russki* and Vera would get angry at herself for not having learned more Russian at the Language Larder. For example, when they met and hugged each other on the street, Daddy said, *"Privetik, zhopa."* She thought *privetik* was a form of *privet,* a standard greeting, but whatever the second word was it must have been very naughty, judging by Daddy's tone.

"Kak dela, suka?" the Seal said, which, Vera guessed, followed the same format of greeting and jolly insult.

The Seal's name actually came from a language joke Daddy had made. The Seal had taught literature for several decades at a college called Tulane. After all those years in New Orleans he joined another organization called AA, which forbade him to have any fun, and he and Daddy were "estranged"—"i.e.," had become strangers. But now he was living across the river, teaching at a community college (I HATE TEACHING, the bumper sticker on his old non-self-driving Volvo read) and "back at it big time" re: fun. In any case, "Tulane" sounded very much like the Russian word *tulen,* which meant "seal," and Daddy's tall, glossy, and chubby friend resembled, in Daddy's words, a "handsome post-Soviet Ashkenazi seal." He even had the whiskers that went along with the nickname and Vera could readily picture him lying "indolently" on a rock and sunning himself as he mumbled "sweet nothings" about "homoerotic Soviet literature," of which he believed himself to be the "world's foremost and only specialist."

Being immigrants, Daddy and the Seal loved a bargain and on Tuesdays the Spanish restaurant offered carafes of sangria for eight dollars, which to Vera sounded like less than a bargain, even for the merely rich. "Get ready for a long evening, kids," the Seal said as he ruffled Vera's and Dylan's hair. His hand smelled of something delicious, hibiscus maybe, as well as Daddy's special juice, of which sangria constituted a sub-branch. Despite Anne Mom's prohibition of screens, the Seal presented Dylan with his phone, and her brother was lost to them for the rest of the meal. Now was the time for Vera to listen and learn. She knew as the evening progressed Daddy would get "sloppy" and open up to the Seal about Mom Mom's cancer. She only hoped it would happen before they switched to Russian so as to better keep their secrets.

Vera munched on her garlicky *pan con tomate* and equally garlicky razor clams. "Truth be told," she did not like garlic, but if she were to "identify" as Korean she had to learn to love it. Even Standoffish Joon-hee ate homemade kimchi *gimbap* at lunch and Vera wished Anne Mom could master the art of making the rolls, too, although Daddy always praised her WASP lunches, while labeling mayonnaise and lettuce the "culinary standard-bearer of Five-Three."

As the first carafe was downed and the second one "hit

the mat," in Seal "parlance," the adults talked about politics, their voices rising around their table, which was parked in the middle of the sidewalk, the excellent weather settling around them in a weighted blanket of warmth and friendly cheer. "Look at how Daddy and the Seal talk," Anne Mom would say to Vera. "Look at their body language, so relaxed." "Friendship must get a lot easier when you can start to drink," Vera remarked, and Anne Mom, to her credit, smiled and laughed and looked like she was just about to kiss Vera on the forehead, the way she so naturally did to her son.

"You know, more than half of Americans can't read on a sixth-grade level," Daddy was saying. "How are you supposed to have a democracy with statistics like that? We lead the developed world in basic illiteracy."

"I read at a ninth-grade level," Vera proudly declared, taking an "adult" sip of her fizzy apple juice.

"Shit, someone make this girl Five-Three," the Seal said.

"I'm Five-Three!" Dylan shouted in the middle of his videogame and through a mouth stuffed with *patatas bravas.*

"Don't let your mom hear you say that," Daddy said.

"Busted!" the Seal said. He didn't have children but liked to "lower himself" to their level, according to Anne Mom.

Daddy started to "pontificate" about what would happen after the constitutional conventions passed Five-Three.

He sounded like he was on television. He even sometimes turned to look out of the corner of his eye because he liked to be "recognized," but the people at the adjoining table were just "a bunch of tourists" who did not appreciate the intellectuals in their midst.

"We'll be part managed democracy, part mixed theocracy, like Israel or Iran," Daddy was saying. "Elements of religious fundamentalism will be in constant tension with the remnants of postdemocracy."

"How is that any different from today?" the Seal asked.

("See that," Vera heard Anne Mom saying. "Back and forth they go, like Ping-Pong. Each one knows what will make the other laugh.")

"Yeah," Vera said. "Seriously, how is that any different from today?"

The adults smiled at her with their red teeth. "You, my *sladkaya*, are so very, very cute," the Seal said. Vera knew that *sladkaya* meant "sweet one" in Russian; it was what Baba Tanya and Grandpa Boris said on the rare occasions she got to visit them (her paternal grandparents were never vaccinated against the last virus and were afraid to venture outside their home).

It was nice to be called sweet and cute, but this also meant that she was, at best, at the stage of Dylan, who was bathed in those kinds of compliments by everyone on the planet, even passersby. She wanted to surpass Dylan, to prove that she was the one who was exceptional.

"Brass tacks," the Seal was saying, "what does all this mean for a Jewish homo like me? Is it time to pack my bags for Kreuzberg? I really don't believe in 'staying and fighting.' A buddy of mine teaches techno music studies at Humboldt in Berlin. I could do my schtick there, too, I bet. I check many boxes for the Germans."

"As long as you don't get checked in to any boxcars *by* the Germans," Daddy said and they both laughed "uproariously."

"More sangria!" the Seal was shouting at the "harried" waiter.

The evening escalated and the tourists were now staring at the laughing and shouting middle-aged men enjoying their friendship, staring at them with what Daddy would call "class enmity." Maybe they were Five-Three and had children who wore overalls and were covered with grime like the fire extinguisher that wouldn't extinguish any fire at school. Vera's monkey brain was "racing." She wanted someone to talk to her and to get some of her words out, but Daddy and the Seal had now switched to Russian and their conversation was growing more somber, because that's what Russian did to you. Her teacher, the other Vera, had never once smiled, even when reading the ostensibly funny book about a clumsy bear who failed to live by the complex rules of forest society and constantly needed to learn *distsiplina* (discipline) from his animal peers. "We can all use some more *distsiplina*," Teacher Vera would say.

"It is what our *vozhd'*"—or "leader"—"expects from us."
Then she would show them the photograph of a man who
looked like a sad but disciplined hamster in a suit in front
of a tricolor flag.

Several times she thought she heard Daddy say "Irak"
while sighing. Vera tried to parse that word and it scared
her. She used to have a poster with the Russian alphabet
explained through pictures of animals. *R* was *rak,* a cray-
fish, a kind of unimpressive lobster common to Russia. But
Daddy had also taught her that *rak* meant "cancer" in
Russian. The word *i* meant "and" so maybe Daddy was
saying "and cancer" while sighing. "Her real mom is missing *and cancer* she has." Well, that didn't make any sense.
Maybe he was actually saying "Iraq," the Mesopotamian
country her brother couldn't spell right.

"I'm learning about cancer in science class!" Vera said.
It was not like her to lie, but she couldn't stand it any longer. "Thank God we don't know anyone who has it."

Her daddy looked at her, but in addition to his surprise
at her utterance she thought there was the same sadness in
his eyes as when the subject of his own parents came up.
Sad and scared, she thought. Just like me. Oh, Daddy.

"What did Lenin say?" the Seal asked. *"Uchitsa, uchitsa,
uchitsa!"* Vera knew that this was from a verb which meant
"to study" (hence "Study, study, study!"), but she wished
for a moment that the Seal and Daddy wouldn't just make
a joke out of everything.

"Oh, shit," Daddy said. "It's past bedtime and your mom is going to kill me."

"She doesn't care," Dylan said from his videogame. "She's got her anti-Five-Three thing."

"Your mommy is a blondish Rosa Parks," the Seal said and they laughed some more.

"No back of the bus for Anne Bradford," Daddy said.

"Or any fucking Anne," the Seal said. "Come on, let's whip out our pens."

This was the hobby the Seal and Daddy shared, though only Daddy was a manfluencer.

"Look at the golden nib on this son of a bitch," Daddy said. "Bet it writes smooth as fuck." When Daddy played with pens, he was "genuinely" happy, Vera thought. He didn't even bother to mind his language.

9

An interesting thing happened in the elevator back home. Inside it was the famous podcaster and her "roommate slash girlfriend" and the two of them were kissing when she and Daddy and Dylan ran in. Vera had never seen two people kiss so "full of passion." Their mouths were on each other even though the podcaster's was covered with lipstick and she was getting it on the other woman's chin, and their eyes were open all the while, which she had overheard Moncler Ada say one should never do if someone were to kiss you. Vera put her hand to her stomach and suddenly wanted to pee.

Daddy began to talk to the women using so many tough words she might have needed a second volume of the *Things I Still Need to Know Diary*. Vera couldn't concentrate on what he was saying, but it was about an anti-gay law in Idaho or thereabouts and Daddy was very sober-seeming and made many points with his index finger. But unlike many people, the two women in the elevator did not really respond to Daddy beyond a few nods. It's almost like they did not want Daddy to be there and probably didn't even want him on a podcast. For once, Vera wanted to share a social cue with Daddy. Stop talking, she wanted to say. Let them keep kissing. Like maybe you once kissed with Mom Mom, so "full of passion."

"Some people just aren't very nice," Daddy said when they entered their apartment, the living room now strewn with the kind of "cheap" political literature Daddy detested. He sounded like a ten-year-old when he said it.

"I'm sorry, Daddy," Vera whispered. She wanted to remind him that Bloomberg thought he was a "man we might need to take seriously," but Anne Mom huffed in and very loudly declared it to be bedtime.

8.

She Had to Survive the Revenge of Miss Campari

The unthinkable happened in Miss Campari's class. Word had gotten back to her that Vera had raised the "one to the power of zero" question in Ms. Tedeschi's class and that the Internet had proven Vera right and Miss Campari wrong. As revenge, Miss Campari had thrown a quiz, even though school had only started days ago, and she deducted enough points from Vera for not "showing her work" that she ended up with the equivalent of a B grade. The "impromptu" quiz would count for twenty percent of their total grade, Miss Campari declared, her posture so straight that Moncler Stephen and some of the other boys gasped for reasons they could not yet fully explain. Vera gasped, too. Now she would never be a woman in STEM.

"It's not fair." Vera was crying at home. "I hate Miss Campari!"

"Miss Campari?" Daddy said. "Sounds like she needs a drink."

"Please shut up, Igor," Anne Mom said, her use of his given name meaning she was also distressed.

"I got a B in math, too!" Dylan shouted.

"On your math *homework*," Vera shouted back, "and only because I did half of it."

"Still, we both got the same grade," Dylan said proudly.

Vera didn't know how it happened, but within seconds she had slapped Dylan clear across his face.

"Vera!" both of her parents shouted. And then Dylan was holding his hand up to his cheek and crying "inconsolably."

"He's faking!" Vera shouted. "He and Stephen slap each other on the playground all the time! He hits me on the elbow every time we pass the Octagon." But Daddy and Anne Mom had their arms around Dylan in full "you're the meat and we're the buns" mode. Daddy had even put down his phone. "Go to your room, Vera," Anne Mom said in her scariest "tired" voice. "Take my phone and do at least ten minutes of meditations."

Instead of letting the warm liquid flow through her body while the man with the English accent taught her to become a vessel for nothingness, Vera took Kaspie out of his drawer and they played game after game, Vera not even noticing if she was winning or losing. She could still hear Dylan pretending to cry out on the Maginot Line and she knew he loved being the "metaphorical" hamburger meat, which he would always be, while Vera's best hope was to become a soggy bun.

It had been nice for Anne Mom to raise her after Mom Mom had abandoned her and after she and Daddy found each other, but Vera was nothing more than a "stopgap measure" for Anne Mom until Dylan popped out like "a little golden gift" (according to Grams in Maine) "with the most darling eyelashes." "He looks very European," Baba Tanya had observed, "almost like a Norwegian."

"I got a B in math today," Vera said to Kaspie.

"That is very sad, but I am sure you can do better," Kaspie said. "Your parents expect very much from you."

"Daddy says he has the connections to get me in Swarthmore and Dylan into Colgate, but with a B in math it might not be feasible." She liked using the word "feasible."

"Our parents invested so much into us," Kaspie said. "They have died a thousand deaths for us."

"Like your Professor Oh," Vera said. "How highly ranked is the Korea Advanced Institute of Science and Technology?" She put a bishop she had just lost to Kaspie between her teeth, which was "unsanitary." Grams's daddy had been a bishop in the Anglican church. It was where Anne Mom got some of her "holier-than-thouness," according to Daddy.

"It is ranked first for science and technology," Kaspie said. "Like MIT."

"Wow," Vera said. "No wonder you keep beating me."

"Swarthmore is ranked number four among national liberal arts colleges," Kaspie said. "It is nothing to sneeze at."

"Oh, I'm not sneezing," Vera said.

"I believe it is an expression."

Vera laughed. "I'm going to write that down," she said. "How is Colgate ranked?"

"Twenty-first among national liberal arts colleges."

"Daddy must think I'm a lot smarter than Dylan," Vera said.

Although her parents both insisted that where one went to college did not matter, they certainly talked about colleges a lot. Anne Mom was legendary for her BA and master's from Brown, but Daddy had gone to a place he called the College of Fading Repute in the "great state of Ohio." That's where he first met Mom Mom, although a long while had passed before Mom Mom gave birth to Vera. They had to first "reconnect" in the city, which Vera pictured (not entirely incorrectly) as an old-fashioned thumb drive being slid into a laptop.

"No flipping pressure," Daddy had once said to her and Dylan on the subject of the College of Fading Repute, "but if either one of you end up going there, I'll take out my eye with a peashooter." Vera had been so stunned by the statement she had "blurted out," "Which eye?" But it was only Daddy's famous sarcasm.

Still, she had to get into Swarthmore and Dylan into Colgate because Daddy wanted to tell people that both his kids had gone to public school yet ended up in excellent liberal arts schools with low "student-to-faculty ratios." Their entire family would look great if that happened. "But I hate brushing my teeth," Dylan said when told of his future alma mater. "You're going to be the president of your frat," Daddy had told him. Dylan considered this honor, then dropped his pants and screamed, "Look at my penis!" "See, you're halfway there," Daddy had said.

As Vera thought about how much was expected of her and how little of her brother, who would be sent to the toothpaste school probably to become a dentist, she grew more and more irate.

"I hate my family!" she said as Kaspie forked her queen and remaining rook.

"Family is everything," Kaspie said solemnly.

"Anne isn't even my real mom," Vera said.

"How do you mean?" Kaspie asked.

Vera explained her origins to the chessboard. She even mentioned that her birth mom was Korean. "Oh," Kaspie said. He didn't have a face, but Vera could tell he was "visibly" stunned. She had told him she was Korean before but never mentioned the particulars of her mom mom.

After a few more moves in which he cleaned up on her pawns, he said, "You must find her."

She put her hand to her prominent cheekbones. "Why do you think?"

"She is your mother. She is Hanguk-*saram*. Korean person."

"Yes," Vera said. "I must."

There was a "perfunctory" knock on the door and then the door opened and it was Anne Mom. Had she overheard her and Kaspie? The thought was unbearable.

Anne Mom sat down next to Vera on the bed and put her arm around her shoulder. She smelled sweaty. "About what happened," she began.

"I'm sorry!" Vera shouted.

"We don't hit," Anne Mom said in her best granddaughter-of-a-bishop (or was it a vicar?) voice. "But I'm also sad that you got a B despite trying so hard. Although, as I've said, grades don't matter." The last two statements seemed contradictory to Vera. "In any case, I'm going to go talk to the principal."

"You're going to get me a higher grade?" Vera asked.

"No, because grades don't matter," Anne said.

Vera was confused. "But how will I get into Swarthmore?" she asked.

Anne Mom sighed. Once again, she had the look of the woman on the stand of the WILL SUFFERING END? church ladies. Maybe it was time to walk to the pharmacy for her special vitamins. "Listen," she said. "I know sometimes you feel ignored in comparison with Dylan, but that's just because you're already so smart and mature."

"I'm not mature," Vera said. "I have social issues."

"Those will straighten out by college," Anne Mom said.

"Unlike Dylan's ADHD?"

"I want you to have fun, honey. You said Yumi invited you for a playdate?"

"A debate practice."

"Even better. That provides you with a ready-made discussion topic. I just talked about what happened with Aunt Cecile and she said she's going to come over and help you practice some more. You can even go for a walk and maybe do some shopping at the vintage store. No new clothes, okay? They're made by slaves in Bangladesh."

"Yay!" Vera shouted. It was as if her "burdens" had been "lifted," per the church ladies. "Can I get a haircut with Aunt Cecile?" she asked Anne Mom.

"Why? Your hair looks great."

"I have to accentuate my cheekbones."

Anne Mom laughed and put a hand on one of Vera's cheekbones. Her hand was so dry. "Okay, honey," she said.

9.

She Had to Kiss Aunt Cecile

"Aunt C., what's a thirst trap?"

They were walking through their neighborhood, which Daddy liked because there was nothing "she-she" about it. Indeed with its "profusion" of jungle gyms it seemed built for a boy like Dylan. She chided herself for thinking in binaries again.

Aunt Cecile laughed. She was pretty short for an adult, though of course not as short as Vera. Anne Mom was very tall, taller than Daddy, who had to make up for this deficiency with a fountain of "sparkling wit." She had read as much when she peeked into a copy of his collection of personal essays, *Kindertransport*, one insomniac night.

"It's when you really like how someone looks," Aunt Cecile said. "Do you think someone's a thirst trap? Someone in school?"

"No. But Joon-hee thinks Stephen's a thirst trap. Probably because of his statuses."

"Well, then she's using it all wrong. You know someone's a thirst trap when you see them. It's not about statuses." Vera thought of the two women kissing in the elevator and put her hand to her own stomach. They were so thirsty for each other, Vera thought, like when they climbed the Seongsan Ilchulbong on Jeju Island and there were no stands selling bottles of water like there would be back home. That's how thirsty the podcaster and her roommate were.

At the thrift store she picked out a kind of junior version of Ms. Tedeschi's sundress with very she-she-looking European women holding umbrellas under rain pours. (Perhaps it would improve her grade if she wore it, Vera couldn't help but think.) "Tray Cherbourg," Aunt Cecile said of the women on the sundress. "Or maybe it's the Morton Salt girl." Vera was about to query both statements, but sometimes with Aunt Cecile it was just great to be next to her, to sense her presence without Daddy's famous sarcasm or Anne Mom's web of love and despair.

"It's forty-five dollars," Vera said when Aunt Cecile "whipped out" her card.

"You're worth it, sweets," she said, and just like that she had a new sundress. (Things happened fast with Aunt Cecile.) They went to drink smoothies in a place that also cut hair, which was so white and bare that it fit in with Vera's concept of an afterlife even though she was an atheist. Grams had sent her to Sunday school when they were visiting up in Maine, but she got kicked out when she insisted, very loudly and maybe a little obnoxiously, to Father Chase and the other kids that heaven wouldn't work because of its lack of gravity. "The only time a five-year-old's ever been kicked out," Grams said, not without a touch of pride. "Strong opinions like her dad," she added, though this part sounded less complimentary. Now that her mom mom had cancer, Vera wished Father Chase had talked more about the mysteries of death; although when Vera thought about death "long and hard," she realized, sadly, that it was no mystery at all.

"So," Aunt Cecile said over their blueberry-banana-avocados. "Heard you got a little handsy with the old Dylan today."

"I didn't mean to," Vera said. "I'm sorry. It's because I got a B in math even though I was right and Miss Campari is an idiot. Is it okay if I talk like that?" she asked, knowing the answer.

"Knock yourself out," Aunt Cecile said. "World's full of idiots." Vera noticed the slight hook of Aunt Cecile's nose when she sipped through a straw, very much like Daddy's. She wanted to hug her. "But why are you so upset about getting a B?" Aunt Cecile asked. "I mean, who cares?"

"It'll go on my record," Vera said.

"And then what?"

"Well, when I'm applying to other schools . . ."

"You're applying to other schools?"

"It's just that people will see that I'm a bad student. Being smart is one of the few things I have that I can be proud of."

"You're not proud of the fact that you're kind and curious and pretty?" Aunt Cecile asked. "And a B doesn't make you a bad student."

"Kind and curious and pretty?" Vera repeated. She needed to pee again. The bathroom seat was the kind that felt warm against your legs, like they had back in Korea and Japan. Daddy had promised to get them toilets like that after the Rhodesian Billionaire came through and bought his struggling magazine. Aunt Cecile couldn't have meant the "pretty" part, though, or could she have? She certainly wasn't "kind" to Dylan when she slapped him. "Cecile is too nice," she had overheard Daddy say more than once to Anne Mom. "People that nice usually get flattened by the Zamboni of life like in the cartoons."

Vera beheld her cheekbones after the hair no longer haloed her head but rather hung from it in an aggressive adult fashion like the wave of the tsunami that was supposed to have "flattened" Okinawa last summer. "You look like a model," the man who had cut her hair said, and Aunt Cecile nodded, smiling. The man was very *joon*, or "handsome," but what adults thought and what kids thought were very different. Vera had worn her cool sweatpants to Dress Down Friday at school and had said to Moncler Ada, "Look, I'm bloke core!" "What the hell is bloke core?" Ada had asked. And when Vera didn't know, she laughed and said, "Thanks, Facts Girl." Unfortunately, that was becoming her nickname at school this year. Like there was something wrong with facts.

Still, the way the adults were smiling at her made her feel special. "A few more years," the man said, "and we can add a little blush to those cheeks."

"I can see that," Aunt Cecile said.

They walked over to an old railroad trestle that had been remade into a very she-she park surrounded with apartments owned by the "oligarchs of the world" according to Daddy. Maybe the Rhodesian Billionaire owned one or two, though he probably lived in a town house like Stephen. To get to the trestle you had to take a small glass elevator and Vera found herself crammed in right next to Aunt Cecile. She put her head on her shoulder and enjoyed the way they were squeezed together. You're my human weighted blanket, Vera thought. You're my nightlight.

There were a lot of tourists on the old elevated railroad and Daddy would surely hate most of them for not recognizing that he was special. Vera tried to catch reflections of herself wherever they went—did she really look like a model? A model of what? She *had* been a model student until Miss Campari's B.

There was a kind of wooden mini-auditorium where two railroad tracks met from which you could see the street below, which was perfect for Vera to practice her debating skills for Aunt Cecile. She started to rattle off all the facts she had gathered on Five-Three, but Aunt Cecile stopped and "reset" her just so that she could breathe correctly again, her secret weapon. When she breathed, and with her new hair that accentuated her cheekbones, Vera felt something like "invincible." The arguments she had lined up in front of her came easily and "organically." There were people watching her perform, but it did not matter because they were merely tourists, some probably with poor English like Taiwanese Davis.

Aunt Cecile had her do an acting exercise in which they repeated the sentence "You're wearing a yellow sundress" to each other, even though the sundress was in Vera's recyclable bag and Aunt Cecile was wearing her skinny jeans and a T-shirt that said JOHN DEAR with the picture of a humanoid tractor giving off heart emojis. Vera had to change the pitch of her voice to mimic Aunt Cecile's. "*You're* wearing a yellow sundress." "You're *wearing* a yellow sundress." "You're wearing a yellow sundress?" Now it was a question. Back and forth they went, with Vera "aping" Aunt Cecile "marvelously."

"You're a natural," Aunt Cecile said. "Now do your pro-Five-Three crap, keeping in mind your breathing and the pitch of your voice." She stopped herself. "I'm sorry, you can't think of it as crap when you're doing it."

"But afterward I can?"

"Afterward you must."

"Every biosphere has animals that are going extinct," Vera began, "animals that were responsible for a lot of the original growth of that biosphere. This happens in societies and countries as well." She took a deep breath, then turned to face Aunt Cecile, her audience, to emphasize her point with her index finger. "This is happening *in our country.* White evangelical *Christians* are the about-to-be-extinct *animals* of our society, because nobody really wants to be like them anymore. Five-Three, an enhanced vote for a new marginalized caste"—she had to remember to pronounce it "cast"—"is the only way to save them from complete extinction."

"Oh my God," Aunt Cecile said. "How—" She looked "perturbed." "I mean where did you pick up that information? I mean how can that possibly be true?"

"I think it is true," Vera said. "I heard Daddy saying it."

"Your father was saying it? He must have been super sarcastic."

"No, he was serious," Vera said. "I'm working hard on picking up social cues."

"I know you are," Aunt Cecile said. "But what was the context for him saying that? 'Context' means—"

"I know what 'context' means. He was on a call with the billionaire that wants to buy his magazine. We were driving up to school in Stella."

Aunt Cecile raised her left eyebrow and said nothing.

Her eyebrow is "exiting stage right," Vera thought, as Ms. Tedeschi had endowed them with a little bit of stagecraft for the debate. Just wait till she "busted out" her own sundress.

"This is all very interesting," Aunt Cecile finally said.

"Please don't get Daddy in trouble with Mom," Vera said. "He's already in the doghouse. Although, I guess, she's in his doghouse, too." Vera laughed. "The funny thing is that we don't even own a dog. Although Daddy calls me Doxie."

She began to chatter on with her monkey brain, until Aunt Cecile pressed her close to her and petted the remains of her hair. This lasted for at least one gorgeous minute. When Vera came out of Aunt Cecile's embrace she saw that the sun was setting over the river (Japan was the Land of the *Rising* Sun, so the West was clearly in the other direction) and that despite all of her thoughts the world was coloring beautifully, the red lights on the butts of the cars below them all gearing up at the stoplight to go uptown, the steady hum of the awful tourists who were now not so awful with all of their languages intertwined like a street pretzel that no one would ever buy her, and the seeming eternity of the glass buildings lined up against the railroad trestle, their "units" dark into the night because the oligarchs were elsewhere doing their horrible oligarch things, but they had left the city these empty towers like a gift, like the gifts of the Magi Grams in Maine had once told her about when she was just three, when Grams looked into the thoughtful brown of her complicated eyes, her hands on the cutting board making edible squares of a WASP sandwich.

All of this, plus the residual coconut smell of Aunt Cecile's hair, touched Vera, and she, in turn, touched her own stomach and wondered where the nearest bathroom was so that she could pee, and she could picture herself doing it in a way that was very pleasurable, though she couldn't quite quantify or qualify (and she was good at both) why it would be so pleasurable. She was thinking now of the podcaster and her roommate kissing in the elevator and it seemed like a very big event—"epochal," as Ms. Tedeschi had said of the constitutional conventions. But somehow their love was even larger than that. How could she communicate any of that to Aunt Cecile? And yet she felt that she had to.

"Isn't this romantic?" she said, gesturing to the street below them and the glass above.

"Yes, it is," Aunt Cecile said.

She took a deep breath. "Should we kiss?" she asked. As she said it, she knew it was wrong, verging on terrible, verging on punishable. But Aunt Cecile held her chin, the way the podcaster had held her roommate's, and then placed a kiss on one and then the other cheekbone. Vera wanted to cry out in gratitude, but "held her tongue." Still, as wonderful as the cheekbone kisses were, she wanted to touch Aunt Cecile's lips with her own. She began to move her head forward, her eyes closed as Moncler Ada had instructed, but here Aunt Cecile took her by the shoulders and turned her around so that they both faced the amphitheater of the street, where she had just done so well at debating.

"I'm sorry," Vera whispered.

"There's nothing to be sorry for," Aunt Cecile said. "You're lovely. What a life you will have. Despite everything."

"When I get older, we'll have more to talk about," Vera said, though what she really meant was the possibility of kissing her lips.

"I don't want you to get older," Aunt Cecile said. "I know that's terrible."

"Why not? How else will I improve?"

"I don't want you to improve. Sorry, that's wrong. You should improve. It's just that you're so perfect. So perfect for me. Such a perfect friend." She was talking to her, but her eyes were elsewhere.

"What if I become a Tradwife like some people?" Vera asked.

"You won't," Aunt Cecile said.

"Because I lack the capital?"

"I don't want to get older either," Aunt Cecile said, "apropos" of nothing, or maybe something. She kept staring out at the delectable "cornucopia" of cars below them, everyone in such a hurry to leave downtown. It was like the one book Vera always had to put front and center when Anne Mom's friends came, *Their Eyes Were Watching God*. Only, only these were Aunt Cecile's singular eyes. And there probably was no God.

"You're not that old!" Vera said to break up Aunt Cecile's fugue.

"I'm not," Aunt Cecile said. "That's what's so sad about it, I guess. Or so they say."

"Sad about what?" Vera asked. "Sad about what?" she demanded again. "Who is saying it?" But Aunt Cecile merely wiped her "God-watching" eyes and stood up so that she was still taller than Vera. "It got cold fast tonight," she said. And then in her actor's voice, she said, "Brrr."

10.

She Had to Be Cool in Front of Yumi

The weekend came and it was resolved between Anne Mom and Yumi's mom that Vera was to travel to Yumi's apartment overlooking the other river for debate practice. Although Anne Mom had "a lot on her mind" re: her own fundraiser, she took this "playdate slash debate practice" very seriously, as she had always eyed Yumi as a potential friend for Vera.

She sat Vera down on the Maginot Line couch and spoke in the same diction as Father Chase of the Maine Sunday school. "Don't get overexcited," she said. "Don't get overheated. Yumi's a nice girl. Very patient. She's the daughter of diplomats, so she has to be. I think her sister has some social-emotional difficulties so she has experience with kids who are different. I know you want to sound cool and adult, but remember, Yumi's not an adult. She's just a great child. And you're a great child, too?"

Perhaps Anne Mom hadn't meant to ask it as a question, but Vera readily answered, "I am." To demonstrate her comprehension, she added, "I'm just a kid."

"Always think, Is this an appropriate thing to say or not? This is a skill your father hasn't fully mastered."

"I can hear you," Daddy sang from the kitchen.

"When you talk to someone on their level, you're doing them a favor. And then you're doing yourself a favor because you're making a friend."

"Gotcha," Vera said, although she sounded very adult when she said it.

"And I have some good news," Anne Mom said. "I spoke to Principal Bellavista and we negotiated your math grade up to an A minus!"

"Wow!" Vera shouted. This was good news "indeed," but she didn't say that because it would be inappropriate language for a mere child who was about to go on a playdate.

"But remember that grades don't matter."

"Of course not."

Anne Mom sighed. "I may not have the gumption of some of those Asian moms on the PTA," she said, "but I try."

"Racist much?" they heard Daddy from the kitchen.

Vera knew that Anne Mom detested being called a racist as much as she hated being called a Tradwife. She had been born "Ann" but added the *e* to her name after reading the diary of Anne Frank, a Jewish girl killed by the

Nazis, as a tween. Now for certain, a terrible fight would break out. But Anne Mom held her tongue probably because she wanted Vera's playdate to go well and did not wish to upset her. Anne Mom's predictability was one of the things Vera liked most about her.

❦

Yumi lived exactly twenty blocks north and five blocks east of Vera's apartment. She pictured Kaspie moving a knight from one apartment to the other. Twenty to the power of five was 3.2 million, which she had once heard was the "floor" in investible assets to make a person or a household be considered "merely rich." She had to stop her mind from racing, because otherwise her tongue would follow.

"Have fun," Anne Mom said sadly to Vera as she handed her over to Yumi's mom. Yumi's family lived in an apartment that resembled Vera's in "broad strokes," but it was a bit smaller and the bedrooms were all clustered together without a Maginot Line, which maybe was why Yumi looked so well rested after not suffering from insomnia from being alone at night. Yumi's mommy and daddy were diplomats, which probably meant that the apartment was a rental and did not contribute to their net worth. It was minimally furnished, but there were signs of "Japaneseness" all over the place, especially the calligraphy on the walls.

"That's my daddy's hobby," Yumi explained, following Vera's eyes.

"My daddy collects fine engraved fountain pens," Vera said, sensing a "common interest" between their two daddies that could "blossom" into a friendship if properly "cultivated."

"I think calligraphy is done like with an inkwell and a brush," Yumi said. "But fountain pens sound very cool, too." She was so nice.

"It's exciting that you girls are going to debate together," Yumi's mom said in a strong but understandable accent. "Yumi really appreciates your intelligence, Vera. You will be a great team together!" She was even smaller than Aunt Cecile and had a haircut that was very similar to Vera's new one.

"It's a Lincoln–Douglas debate," Vera said. "Lincoln debated Senator Douglas, who was in some ways even more progressive than him, especially about slavery. Did you know Lincoln was called the Ape of Illinois because he was tall and hairy?"

Vera stopped talking. This was how she got into trouble. This is how she "overheated." But when she mentioned that Lincoln was the Ape of Illinois, Yumi made an ape sound and pretended to scratch under her armpits and her mother laughed "gregariously" and brought a hand up to her mouth. "Such funny girls," she said. All of this was making Vera feel at home, especially the smell of fish coming from the kitchen, which made her nostalgic for something she couldn't identify. But then she could. Yumi's mother was Asian like her own had been. Or still was. Or something. She hated that happiness and sadness were always forming a pretzel.

Vera knew that Yumi's younger sister really looked up to her, even though she was not good enough to get into their school. So she was taken aback by a sign on Yumi's bedroom door that read NO SISTERS ALLOWED. But then she realized this was humor, a kind of American humor she did not expect from Yumi's family. Her own family, she knew, was not fully American because Daddy brought an "immigrant's aesthetic" to it. But next to the sign, someone had used crayons to draw a picture of two girls with black hair, their stick arms around each other. Her sister must have been the artist. They were a very creative family, and even though they "ribbed" each other, they loved each other.

Inside Yumi's room there were many posters of pop bands that children were supposed to enjoy, a big difference between Vera's blank walls and her woolly "ersatz papa" (a Daddy phrase), Garry Kasparov. Many of these pop bands, she realized, were Korean. During their summer trip Daddy had mentioned that there had been an "enmity" between Japan and Korea, but now it was "more or less" okay. Everything is going to be okay, she told herself.

In addition to the posters, there were several corkboards and whiteboards with both English and Japanese characters upon them. Vera quickly realized that these were a guide to Yumi's schoolwork written in her mother's beautiful handwriting, a "compendium" of homework assignments due, tests to be prepped for, and extracurricular activities to be pursued. And Yumi's mother did all this while still herself pursuing her career as a diplomat! It was no wonder that Anne Mom felt so "outgunned" by the PTA moms. Maybe it was because her "suffering" would never "end," per the sign the religious women had put up. And somewhere, Vera thought, her mom mom was dying of cancer, when instead she could be filling corkboards and whiteboards with Vera's academic and extracurricular life, giving her a hard brittle strength that would make up even for her lack of Five-Three.

"My mommy helped me organize the main points of the debate right here," Yumi said, pointing to a corkboard filled with flash cards. "We can add or subtract whatever we like." She sounded so mature, Vera thought. Perhaps she had to "code switch," as Daddy said of many people, between the mature girl she was at home and the cool friend of Ada and Joon-hee she tried to be on the playground.

"Ms. Tedeschi said we have to think of our opponents' tactics, too, so over here I wrote down all the arguments they might make," Yumi said.

"I'm not worried, Stephen and Davis are pretty dumb," Vera said, trying to sound like she was a Popular at recess. But Yumi smiled and blushed a little. Vera remembered how intently Yumi watched Stephen slap her brother on the playground and get slapped in turn. "I mean, they're not really hero material," Vera said. She couldn't remember where she learned that phrase, but it sounded perfect for the moment.

Yumi turned away to reshuffle some flash cards. "I don't know," she said. "Stephen's kind of cute." Vera couldn't believe Yumi was sharing this kind of "intel" with her, just minutes into their playdate slash whatever. She put her hand to her mouth, the way she had seen Yumi's mother do. So Stephen was a "thirst trap" for Yumi, not just Joon-hee. This was incredible. Did Ada and Joon-hee even know? There was so much she could say right now, but she had to be cool in front of Yumi.

"I mean he does have a lot of statuses," she said.

"I don't care about that," Yumi said. "I think underneath all his dumb stuff he's very suave."

That was an incredibly adult word. How many words did Yumi know and not use at school? Vera's monkey brain went ape. First of all, like Aunt Cecile, Yumi didn't care about statuses. Then again, one day she would have to go back to Japan when her parents' "tour of duty" was over (this made Vera sad), so all the Five-Three stuff wasn't that important to her. But also Yumi thought that there was more to Stephen than "met the eye," just as Anne Mom had thought about Daddy when they first fell in love, even though in the end she was "sorely disappointed" by how little her eye hadn't met. Vera felt like warning Yumi to be careful, but, again, she had to be cool about it.

The girls both looked at Yumi's desk clock at the same time. They knew, instinctively, that they had to get to work and maybe after a few hours of practice they could talk about Stephen as Yumi's potential boyfriend instead of debate opponent. Vera code switched back to being a studious girl. She was amazed by just how many terms Yumi, or perhaps Yumi's mother, had prepared re: the debate. This was where having a diplomat mommy was clearly superior. For example, there were the differences between something being "de jure" and "de facto." That was "mind blowing" in its own right. Still, Vera had the gift of her breathing technique and newly acquired acting skills. She had to remember that she and Yumi were on the same team and were not competing against each other. Suave Stephen and Taiwanese Davis were the enemy.

"Many countries prioritize some of their citizens over others," Vera was saying, using her index finger to make her points for her. "In India, if you're *Hindu*, you have the ultimate say. In China, the *Han* Chinese are the most prominent citizens. In Israel, *Jews* get to decide most policies. Why should *we* be any different vis-à-vis our most exceptional citizens?"

She stopped. Yumi was looking at her with her eyes cool and maybe even "hazy" in a pretty way. She was a pretty girl, for sure. But why was she looking at her like that? "Was that bad?" Vera asked.

"No, sorry," Yumi said. "You say it so well. Like an actress."

"Oh, thanks."

"It's just so weird that you, not Stephen, will be saying that."

"Because he's Five-Three?"

"I guess I'm just sorry you're not," Yumi said. "Or at least not biologically so that it would count."

"That's okay," Vera said. "I'm going to work very hard to get ahead and everything."

"Was your—" Yumi was clearly trying to be diplomatic here. "Was your original mom Asian? Just because—"

"Yeah," Vera said. "We don't know what happened to her. My daddy doesn't like to talk about her." Now she felt shame "coursing" through her body. She knew this was not how Asian families were supposed to be structured. She remembered the pause Kaspie had taken after she "spilled the beans" to him. But she couldn't help but spill more beans. "I think she's very sick," she said. "I think she has cancer."

Yumi stayed silent for a long while. Vera thought she had destroyed everything they had been building together for the last few hours, the excellent debating, the use of "de jure" and "de facto," the secret about Stephen being "suave," all of it. But when Yumi spoke she sounded as adult and advanced as all of the adults Vera knew combined.

"I'm sorry, Vera," Yumi said, and she said it in a way that indicated to Vera that she was and that there was nothing else to say.

Yumi's mother came in with *onigiri* stuffed with fresh salmon and tuna that she had been preparing in the kitchen all the while. She noticed the sad atmosphere in the room and asked, "Is everything okay?"

"Yes!" Yumi said. "We're just exhausted from practicing." She came over to Vera and put her arm around her shoulder. Vera smiled.

"Good. Please eat the *onigiri* and then practice some more."

But after the rice balls were consumed and Vera licked the sesame oil off her fingers in what Baba Tanya would call an "uncultured" way, they ended up shirking their school duties and lying on the floor next to each other, looking up at the slightly pockmarked ceiling. "Maybe you and Stephen can do something," Vera said. It sounded very adult.

"Yes, but he lives in a town house," Yumi said.

"Oh." Vera did not understand. "Oh?" she tried again.

"It would be embarrassing for him to come to our apartment, which is very small and"—Yumi was testing out a word in her mind to make sure it was not too intimidating, the way Anne Mom wanted Vera to do—"temporary."

"Maybe you can go to his house?"

"I might do something wrong," Yumi said. "Town houses are very big."

"Your parents are diplomats. Maybe they can take you to a town house to practice."

Vera sensed Yumi's fishy breath combining with her own in the air above them. In some ways, this was the most incredible thing that had ever happened to her. Aunt Cecile was her "perfect friend," but this was a "peer." And she was, if not a full-fledged friend, then certainly amenable to some form of friendship.

"Where is your mom?" Yumi asked. "I mean your *mom* mom."

She had come up with the same terminology as Vera! "I don't know," Vera said. "And I don't know how to find her."

"We can look her up," Yumi said.

"My other mom won't allow me to use a device except for meditating."

"I have one. Although I'm only allowed four hours of screen time per week."

"I don't even know her full name," Vera said. "But I do know her first name."

"What is it?" Yumi asked.

Vera stared at the pockmarked ceiling until it became blurry to her. Using Mom Mom's name felt like breaking glass in the case of an emergency. After it was done, it could not be undone.

"Iris," she said.

"That's a pretty name."

"Just like the Egyptian goddess," Vera said. "Or the colored part of the eye."

11.

She Had to Survive Anne Mom's Political Thing

Vera skipped down the street from Stella to her school. "La la la la," she sang, a happy, brainless melody. She was "over the moon" about her weekend time with Yumi. Wasn't it crazy that just one person could change your life so? A peer not an adult, she repeated in her mind when she thought of Yumi.

Her standing with Anne Mom had gone up tremendously after she had been returned to her care by Yumi's beaming mom. "They study so nicely together," Yumi's mom had said. "We can't wait to see her again." "I rocked a playdate," Vera told the whole family at dinner and Daddy looked up from his phone with a smile. "Chip off the old block," he had said. ("Big deal," Dylan "opined.")

But in school, Vera became very nervous. Yes, both she and Yumi would have to code switch, but what would hap-

pen if Ada and Joon-hee attacked her at recess? Or if someone made fun of her during class? She had to stay "quiet as
a church mouse" (Grams of Maine) to get through the
day. During recess, she hid in a stall in the girls' room near
the flame-susceptible auditorium so as not to make a fool
of herself, even though it was not "optimal" in terms of
the odors. "So many Leningrad memories," Daddy had
said once after using the facilities. While stuck in the stall,
Vera schemed about a way to bring Yumi and Stephen together. Perhaps all four of them (including Davis) could
have a playdate to practice a debate. But that would be
conspiring with the enemy.

"Hey, where've you been all day?" Yumi asked her before Ms. Tedeschi's class began.

"Oh, here and there," Vera said "nonchalantly," resist-
ing the urge to throw her arms around Yumi's neck.

9

She had another "stressor" in her life and that was Anne
Mom's political salon. The whole weekend had been leading up to it and now it was here. Things were a bit messy.
On the day before the event, Daddy had to go to Wisconsin to give a speech to some "calorie-rich Americans" for a
"fat" fee. (Many of Daddy's jokes ended up eating themselves.) "Get ready for some amazing farts when I come
back," Daddy told Dylan, re: Wisconsin being "America's
Dairyland." "I'm gonna smoke y'all out of this place."

"I'll eat your farts and become an even bigger farter!" Dylan said. (I hate my life, Vera thought.)

Mommy kept checking Daddy's flight schedule to make sure he would return in time for her thing, because he was the "headliner." "Your anxiety is contagious," Daddy said as he slung his "hipster" satchel over his breast and headed for the airport.

Daddy got back on time, but instead of farts he gave off a more "ponderous" odor. "I got to go to the club to meet some people," he had said. "This could be decisive." Vera knew he was talking about the Rhodesian Billionaire and whether they would be comfortable or not.

"Don't drink too much," Anne Mom had said. "I want you cogent for tonight."

"Yeah, fuck you," Daddy said, which did not improve the atmosphere around the apartment one bit. Even Dylan was in a bad mood and was dying to hit Vera's elbow but knew Anne Mom would not stand for it, not today.

Daddy's club was one of his special places and Vera was desperate to visit and have drinks in one of its "hollowed" rooms. The club looked out on a beautifully manicured private garden that you could "access" with a key from the club. Daddy hated the private park on account of he was "of the left," but he also used it frequently to escape from Anne Mom. Vera always thought it was a great honor to have Daddy take her (but not Dylan) for a walk in the park, where everything was so exclusive and there was a birdhouse that looked like it was meant for a pterodactyl.

She wished very much that things would go right for Daddy at the club, but she was also a "realist."

⸘

"Well, here goes nothing," Anne Mom said and dabbed at her makeup with a napkin. The dining room table, never big, was now drowning in cheeses and hummus and little orange meatballs and spears furnished with olives and anchovies and little green peppers (disgusting, as far as Vera was concerned). More importantly, there was a bartender in a vest who had set up a stand near the kitchen from which he hawked a "medley" of free drinks. ("And it was *my* drinking that was supposed to have bankrupted us," Daddy "slyly" remarked when he heard there would be a costly bartender.) The Maginot Line was covered with cheap folding chairs from the basement that their cooperative used during annual meetings. Even those had to be paid for, Anne Mom had said very angrily. On the chairs, Vera had to place an anti-Five-Three pamphlet and a little thing with a code that you scanned to give money. Practical Vera hoped the money would pay for all the drinks and orange meatballs and cheeses before being given against Five-Three and also why couldn't Daddy bring some extra cheese back from the dairy state?

Next, Vera did another survey of the bookshelves, pulling out *Their Eyes Were Watching God* so that it would be visible from any angle and giving the spine of *The Power Broker* a few good cracks. "I hope you're getting a lot of allowance money for this," Aunt Cecile, another helper, told her.

"I'd rather get a little screen time," Vera said, hoping Anne Mom would hear.

"Not right now," Anne Mom said as she did battle with a faulty halogen light.

"Let me help you," the mustached bartender-in-a-vest said. He looked very suave and he and Aunt Cecile looked at each other as if they were both unquenchable thirst traps.

❧

The event began, but Daddy was still at his club, hopefully not drinking too much. The seats and the couches were all full, and some young people—"activists," they were called—even stood against the walls with their free drinks and orange meatballs. Vera and Dylan were both placed in Vera's room, but they peeked out a lot and Dylan especially loved to run out to grab a skewer or something and then be petted on the head and told how cute he was by one of Anne Mom's friends who, Aunt Cecile told her, had a huge appreciation for shoes called ballet flats. The women in ballet flats all looked like they probably had

Five-Three status, so it was especially nice for them to come to Anne Mom's fundraiser for those who didn't.

Vera was allowed to watch the "proceedings" despite the occasional adult language, because Anne Mom thought this would help her with her debate and her ongoing befriending of Yumi. A lot of people talked about how Five-Three was going to end democracy and there was even a screen showing pie charts and bullet points on strategy. There was a full professor from the fancy university uptown—where Daddy sometimes taught a class "for peanuts"—who was much beloved by the young activists against the wall, who, for some reason, snapped their fingers instead of clapping. A minor politician from across the river said a lot of scary things were happening in his supposedly "idyllic" suburb and it wasn't just the MOTHs, it was other things, "insidious" things. Vera thought he was very handsome and should have been a "power broker" instead of Robert Moses, who looked like a broken Pez dispenser on the cover of the book about him. Anne Mom periodically looked at her phone and at the door as if that would make Daddy appear, but he did not appear. She was drinking a lot of white wine herself, which Vera knew would be a "recipe for disaster."

"Where's Daddy?" even Dylan asked her back in her room. "Is he still drinking at the club?" He was ruffling through all the old books with Asian characters Anne Mom had bought her to make Vera feel good about herself when she was younger. Vera couldn't believe Dylan was actually reading or pretending to read *Jasmine Ho, Teenage Architect*, that's how nervous her brother was.

"It's okay," Vera said. She knew if she put her arm around her brother he would find a way to hit her, so she had to use her words. "They're going to stay together," she said. "I've been working on it."

Dylan looked up at her with Anne Mom's clear blue eyes. "Yeah?" he said. "Maybe I should run into the room and show them all my penis. That'll take the heat offa Daddy."

"That's very funny," Vera said. The siblings looked at each other as if they were two dogs in the street that had never met. Or at least that's how it felt to Vera. "But you shouldn't," she said.

And then they heard Anne Mom giving a speech in the living room and they both peeked out.

Anne Mom was talking loudly and her chest was puffed out in front of her and her voice was breaking as she spoke until it sounded like she was fighting with Daddy and Daddy had gotten the upper hand.

"What did we do when they took away abortion rights fewer than five hundred miles away from us?" Anne Mom asked the assembled. "When Cycle Through got started fewer than four hundred miles from us? We thought the pain of what was happening in this country wouldn't come to our doorstep. But it has."

The activists were now snapping their fingers "in tandem." Some of them were the grown children of Anne Mom's friends in the ballet flats or the more interestingly dressed women from her Brown years. Vera wondered if she would be up against the wall later in life, snapping her fingers alongside them. Was this also expected of her, along with Swarthmore? Where would Yumi be at that point? Back in Tokyo making *onigiri* for her family? Maybe she should move there too now that there was no more enmity between the Japanese and the Koreans. Maybe that would be her Kreuzberg. Just her and her new best friend. She shuddered in happiness and worry at the term. Best friend. It wasn't true, was it? But what if it was?

When Anne Mom finished her wonderful and very powerful speech, many people came up to hug her and, Vera hoped, to donate to her cause and pay for all the hummus. Anne Mom was something of a power broker herself tonight. But why wasn't Daddy here to celebrate with her? Why wasn't he here to "headline"?

After the speech at least an hour passed and nobody knew whether to stay or go. Aunt Cecile and Anne Mom locked themselves in Vera's bathroom and Vera heard Anne Mom yelling, "You call him! You effing call him! I bet he'll come for you!"

After there was almost nothing left to drink, Anne Mom declared to her audience that Daddy was stuck in Wisconsin, a terrible flight delay, which Vera knew was not true.

She desperately wanted to flap her arms, but she didn't want Dylan to see, especially since he was being such a good, quiet little brother, probably scared to death himself of what would happen between his parents.

Soon the room was empty except for the women in ballet flats snapping shut the folding chairs, and each snap felt to Vera like a reproach against marriage and love. When they were gone, Anne Mom and Aunt Cecile sat on the couch, eyeing the door. After a while, Dylan was put to bed and Aunt Cecile left with a ruffle of Vera's new hair and a cheap nervous kiss on one cheekbone but not the other and then Anne Mom was left on the couch all alone.

Vera almost hoped that Daddy wouldn't come home. Not tonight.

12.

She Had to Survive the Night

She had a "front-row seat" to the fight when Daddy finally stumbled home, because he and Anne Mom had chosen the Maginot Line as their battlefield.

"I lost everything!" Daddy was screaming. "All my dreams! All our fortune! Our last chance! And you don't give a fuck!"

"I don't give a fuck? Who kisses your ass and tells you you're the best, the smartest, so fucking brilliant you're allowed to be above the fray, allowed to have a 'persona' instead of a soul?"

"Oh, thanks so much. Thanks for all that cheering. Thanks for all that Christmas good cheer. You should go join the staff at that cheerleader café we saw in Tokyo. At least then you'd have a job."

There was a loud crash and drunken Daddy had fallen over a very expensive coffee table, made out of an African tree, without quite breaking it. Now he was lying on the floor holding on to one leg and making a whiny howl. "Here's your phone," Anne Mom said, throwing the device at his chest. "Call 911 yourself, if you'd like." Then she turned and looked in the direction of Vera's Leperarium. Vera scrambled to get into her bed. Anne Mom leaned into the room; now she was the one who smelled like metal on a hot day. Vera wondered if she should pretend to snore, but Anne Mom soon left, the door closing very gently behind her.

⁹

Vera stayed in that position for a long time, her legs huddled into her stomach, unable to breathe, unable to flap, as if someone were hovering over her, an evil spirit. There wasn't a MOTH that night, but she didn't care if someone did break in through the fire escape to stab her, stab all of them. If they survived it, maybe Daddy would get to go on the news again. He would clearly need a lot of attention to get his self-esteem back. If anyone needed to see Mrs. S., the school counselor with the master's in social work degree, it was Daddy.

A while later—she dared not look at the clock because it would only make her insomnia all the more "written in stone"—she smelled a familiar if peculiar smell. It was coming from the Maginot Line. Was it a fire? You couldn't smell carbon monoxide, so that was good, at least.

Vera pulled tight on her drawstring pajama bottoms. She hugged the picture of Snoopy hugging Woodstock on her night T-shirt and began to make her way to the Maginot Line. Daddy was by the window, his face slightly orange. He was smoking one of his "special cigarettes." This "on top" of the drinking? Vera approached with her bare feet, but it took Daddy a while to notice her.

"Doxie," Daddy said. He had trouble keeping his balance but managed to stub his special cigarette out on the radiator cover as he lowered himself to the parquet floor. "Don't look, baby," Daddy said. At first Vera thought he was talking about not looking at him, but then she realized he had written a bad word on the radiator cover with one of his very fine fountain pens. Daddy laughed. "Hoo boy," he said. "I guess I'm really not hero material tonight."

Vera came close to him, but not close enough for a Snoopy-Woodstock hug. "Are you okay?" she said.

"Do you still love me?" he asked.

"Yes," she said.

"Even though I've fucked everything up. Forgive me. The language out of my mouth."

"Yes," she said.

"You forgive me?"

"Yes," she said.

"And you still love me?" He was repeating himself, but the answer was still yes.

"What is that?" Daddy said. He tried to lift his head up to look out the window, but it was hard for him. "Is there a MOTH tonight?"

"I don't think so," Vera said.

"Sometimes I wish the workers would be brave enough to come up here and punch me in the nose," Daddy said.

"Oh, no," Vera said. How did Daddy know the contents of her worst nightmares?

"Don't worry," Daddy said. "Nobody will ever touch you. Everything I do is for you. Do you know that?"

Vera didn't know that. "Just for me?" she asked. She remembered what Daddy had said during his previous nighttime fight with Anne Mom: "It's not like I'm just walking around the world full of love. I barely have enough for you and the kids." Maybe he only had enough love for Vera? Wouldn't that be wonderful?

"Yeah, your mom and mophead over there will be all right." Daddy waved in the direction of the other bedrooms. "But you and me, we're in this together."

Vera thought about it—maybe she could say what she was about to say and he wouldn't even remember it the next day. That's how it got when Daddy's special juice combined with Daddy's special cigarettes.

"Maybe you and me and *Iris*?" Vera said. "I mean, are in this together."

Daddy was looking into her eyes and there was a little flame inside each of his. She knew this even though it was almost perfectly dark. She had said her mother's name and maybe that had lit the two flames.

"My poor Doxie," Daddy finally said. "Our country's a supermarket where some people just get to carry out whatever they want. You and I sadly are not those people."

"Don't worry about me, Daddy," she said. She turned around on her toes.

"Where are you going? Don't leave me!"

"I won't," she said.

Vera returned with "Six Great Things About Mom and Why You Should Stay with Her."

"I don't have my glasses," Daddy moaned. Still, he read the list with relish, his body giving off great heaves of either sadness or laughter. It was hard to tell which in the dark with only the light of the skyscrapers across the way, the ones that still had living rooms full of intact families and weren't owned by oligarchs like the one who just broke Daddy's heart.

"I love number three," Daddy said, in reference to Anne Mom's "little trust."

"I just don't know how little it is," Vera confessed, hoping for a number.

"Pretty little," Daddy said. "It's been whittled down by time. And arrogance and greed."

"Will it pay for the washer-dryer bills?" Vera asked.

"Just about."

"Are we going to be homeless?"

"In a sense, we're homeless already," Daddy said, and all of a sudden he sounded important, like Miss Campari when she got things wrong.

"Are we going to have to move to Kreuzberg with the Seal?"

"Don't you worry," Daddy said. "No one puts Daddy in the corner." He laughed terribly.

"I just don't want you guys to fight anymore."

"The problem with your mom," Daddy said, "is that she can't get her medication dialed in right."

"Does she need a new phone?" Vera asked. "I've saved up my allowance for Christmas."

But Daddy wasn't listening. "I got some ideas, honey pie," he said. He tapped his head and laughed again. "Pathetic," he said. "I can't be pathetic. You won't sideline me." He was talking to someone invisible at the center of the Maginot Line, someone standing in the middle of the floors Anne Mom and Aunt Cecile had thoroughly scrubbed after everyone and their shoe prints had left. "You won't sideline me," Daddy said again to his mystery guest. "In the right hands even a dick is a balalaika."

Vera didn't know what her father was saying and it worried her. But she didn't know what to say to him and how to make it better. "Doxie," Daddy said after a few moments had passed. "May I ask a favor?"

"Sure, Daddy."

"May I use your bathroom?"

9

Vera heard Daddy "retching" in her bathroom and she knew how painful throwing up could be and it hurt her to see him in so much pain. She wanted to punch the Rhodesian Billionaire right in the mouth with the same force Daddy wanted the workers to use against him. She looked down and she saw little moons of sweat against her Snoopy shirt, another example of her Daddy's inheritance. She thought of a special lane in a supermarket that wasn't even staffed and where nobody had to pay. Anne Mom and Dylan walked right through it with a family-size bag of purple tortilla chips and flaxseed.

When Daddy came out she scrambled into bed and tucked herself in. "Dox?" Daddy said and, although she loved him, right away Vera wished she could open a window because the whole room was filled with many of his smells. She heard him stagger across the room and hit his foot hard against the armoire. It was scary that he didn't even cry out in pain. "Do you mind if I crash with you tonight?" he finally said.

"My bed's big enough," Vera said. "It's a twin." She thought of the Moncler Twins and how lucky they were to live in a normal household with a wealthy father and mother and two sets of stairs. One of the twins was even beloved by Yumi.

Daddy staggered toward the bed and eventually

"crashed" onto one side of it, almost jostling Vera to the floor. "Sorry," he said. He must have noticed the rooks and bishops of her bedcovers because he muttered, "Checkmate." She heard him breathing loudly into her back and shoulders and had to switch to breathing through her mouth.

Still, it felt better in the room with him than without him.

Part Three

●●●

The Next Month

13.

She Had to Spy on Daddy to Figure Out What Was Going On

A darkness had fallen over the Bradford-Shmulkin family that autumn. It was as if the clock had been set back three hours, when it hadn't even been set back one. Everything at home was covered in that darkness, so that even school and even hiding out in the bathroom so as not to be called Facts Girl in front of Yumi seemed like a refuge. (Vera had worn the sundress Aunt Cecile had bought her to Dress Down Friday and Ada had made fun of her for wanting to look like Ms. Tedeschi, even though she wasn't even in that class.)

Daddy didn't do social media, he just lay on the couch in his underwear, his mouth no longer open, the phone hanging limply from his wrist. It was worse than the time Daddy had gotten into a terrible fight with someone named Hannah Arendt, a fight he lost badly despite her being dead. "Let Daddy be Daddy!" she and Dylan sometimes chanted by the couch, but Anne Mom just told them to quiet down and do "their" homework, meaning Vera had to do it for them both.

The only highlight, and it was as high a light as the glowing star atop Grams's famous Christmas tree in Maine, was the time she spent with Yumi, ostensibly practicing their upcoming debate with Thirst Trap Stephen, "et al." She was getting very good at it, with Yumi as an able co-pilot having prepared close to five hundred flash cards with every kind of argument, counterargument, and counter-counterargument. "Stephen Douglas would have loved you," Vera once said, and Yumi just sighed, perhaps pining for her own Stephen, Stephen Wilson of the Clan Moncler. Yumi's mom had even bought them a pair of child-size barristers' gowns and wigs so that they would look like they came from the time of the Revolutionary War, and hence bolster their Five-Three arguments.

But when they weren't practicing their way toward victory and an A plus from Ms. Tedeschi, they were trying to find Mom Mom on Yumi's tablet. The main problem here was that Vera did not know her last name. "When we were in Seoul, Daddy said that most Koreans are named Kim, Lee, or Park," Vera said. "So let's start with those."

But when they searched for Iris Kim, Iris Lee, and Iris Park, they got close to three hundred million results. It seemed that many non-Korean Americans and British-type people also used these last names in combination with "Iris" and that "Lee" was taken by many Chinese people besides. Yumi was so lucky to have a last name like Sae-monsaburou, which was one of the longest Japanese names on record and was written "with over ten kanji letters," according to Yumi.

The only good hint they had about Mom Mom was that she had attended the College of Fading Repute with Daddy, but "Iris" and the college produced no results except for a surgeon who had pioneered some kind of eye surgery back in the day, before the college lost its repute.

"Do you have a Korean name?" Yumi asked her.

"No," Vera said. "I guess my daddy talked my mom mom into giving me a Russian one. They say he can talk the pants off of anyone, whatever that means. My chess-board is Korean, so maybe he can give me a Korean name." She sighed. There were so many things to think about. What if her name wasn't really her name either?

"Well, we're not giving up," Yumi always said after they had failed. "Next week we will try our best again."

Next week. Every time Vera had to shake Yumi's hand goodbye in front of their mothers, she felt like a clock was resetting inside her, waiting for the next weekend to roll around and for her to have a friend again.

9

And then something absolutely "bonkers" happened. Anne Mom left. Not forever, but for a week. She needed to "reboot," and was going to visit Grams in Maine. "Can we come with you?" Dylan whined. "No," Anne Mom said. "You have school. Plus, this is Mommy Time. It can't just be Dylan and Vera Time twenty-four-seven."

"You know we're going to starve to death," Dylan said.

"I've left pages of instructions for your father," Anne Mom said.

"You know he won't read them," Dylan said.

"Well, he's an adult," Anne Mom said.

But Daddy was not pleased by his new parental role, and as Anne Mom left to take a plane to Maine they fought very loudly. "You're a monster," Anne Mom said over the doorstep, "but you're not even a fascinating one like most monsters."

"Aye-aye, Traddy," Daddy said and gave her a very unusual kind of salute.

9

The Reign of Daddy was not an auspicious one. Anne Mom had "predicated" that all rides to school and back in Stella were to be manned by Daddy in the front seat, but Daddy said they were old enough to use an autonomous vehicle. Bereft of adults Stella did fine, although she "aped" Anne Mom's diction all the time. "I'm so *very* tired," she said when the usual battle broke out around the

Octagon. "Great, our exit is closed," she said. "I hate this city so much."

At home, they ate many pizzas, including the disgusting kind Dylan loved with pineapples, three kinds of cheese, and no sauce. "I'm going to fatten you kids up," Daddy said, watching them eat out of the corner of his eye, proud of his ordering skills.

And then another thing started to happen. Daddy started to go away a lot, even after they had gotten home from school. He usually took this time to sprawl on the couch in his underwear, talking to the Seal in a Russian-English patois Vera couldn't understand ("I'm the only *blyad'* they don't allow to fail up in this town"), but now he was going out instead. Vera knew Daddy's magazine had an actual office, but it seemed that most intellectuals like Daddy preferred to work "remotely." So where was Daddy going?

"I gotta work," Daddy would say mysteriously before he left. "Gotta put pineapple pizza on the table. Vera, watch Dylan. You're the man of the house now."

Vera made sure Dylan wolfed down his personal pie and then they sat by the empty couch, Vera doing problem sets with only her hands and eyes, Dylan watching violent cartoons on their noticeably small television.

One day she was playing chess with Kaspie in the bedroom and he asked her how the search for Mom Mom was going. When she told him why it wasn't going well, Kaspie asked why she didn't directly ask her father for Mom Mom's last name. "Is it because he is ashamed?" Kaspie asked. "And you don't want to bring him any further shame because you are a good daughter?"

"Why would he be ashamed?" Vera asked.

"Because he took you from your mother."

"She abandoned me," Vera said, the words much more painful when spoken aloud.

"No sane Korean mother would abandon her child," Kaspie said. "Not in this country with all its wealth."

This really made Vera think. Was Daddy a bad person? Was he keeping her real mother from her? Why would he do that? Was it because he could barely keep a relationship going with Anne Mom? Did he, as Anne Mom once "posited," just "fundamentally hate women"? But Vera herself was going to be a woman one day, a woman in STEM, no less, so how could that be true?

She had a dream one night that Daddy had entered a gigantic room like the Panthéon of the greats they had visited in Paris last year, where Marie Curie, one of the most important women in STEM, was "interred." In the dream, he was there to receive an even-more-special award than the ones England had long-listed him for a long time ago, but all these women had gathered in the "pews" to yell "Shame! Shame! Great shame!" at him. And then a small Asian woman ran up to him and threw a gelatinous narwhal—the kind Dylan and Daddy threw at each other before bedtime—straight into the under-penis part of Daddy, which Dylan referred to, majestically, as his "nuts." When she woke up Vera realized she couldn't remember what Mom Mom's face had looked like in the dream. And then she realized where Daddy must be going all this time. He was not a bad man at all. He was going to visit Mom Mom in the hospital.

❦

Vera had to do something "reckless." It would be so reckless that it could cost her everything re: her family. But then again, how much did she have left to lose with things as they were? She hadn't yet given Anne Mom the list of why she should stay with Daddy, but the other Marriage-Saving List hadn't done much to save the marriage. No, she had to find out what Daddy was up to. She had to spy on him before Anne Mom came back. (Or would she abandon them, too?)

On the next day, when Daddy left for his mysterious rounds, Vera peeked into Dylan's room. Her brother was playing with a sentient phosphorous blob that said things like "Easy, bro," every time he smacked it against the ceiling. "I'll be right back," Vera said to him. "Don't leave the room."

"Later, sucka," Dylan said.

Vera had prepared Anne Mom's emergency key in advance. She locked the apartment door behind her and ran down the stairs as the aging elevator containing Daddy slowly made its way down. She ran down to the basement, out of breath, and opened the door leading out to the street, waiting for Daddy to emerge from the lobby, which he did with a "curt" nod to the doorman.

Vera climbed the basement stairs to street level. She was wearing a hoodie despite the warm weather to hide most of her face. Before her mission she had reread one of the childhood books Anne Mom had given her titled *Yoon-a Choi, Middle-School Spy.* "Remember, Yoon-a," her "handler" (who was also her guidance counselor) said to her in the book, "Now that you're a spy, you're the one who's different. Not the people around you."

And that's how Vera felt now. She was different, but no one could know. She had to be invisible. A short girl walking down the street could attract attention if she made eye contact with a caring adult who would ask her what she was doing out alone. But few caring adults lived in their part of town, according to Daddy. Mostly there were jerks with money, the kind of "sub-oligarchs" who dreamed of yachts but had to content themselves with fountain pens. She followed Daddy down the side street where his club and the private park were located. Daddy had a far-more-brisk walk than she had usually known him to have, and also he wasn't looking at his phone for some reason. Vera tried to think of which hospitals existed nearby, a hospital where Mom Mom could be suffering in pain. She liked to keep a tally of all the hospitals in the vicinity in case anyone was stabbed by a MOTH person or had to be treated for burns because of a faulty fire extinguisher, but she couldn't think of any hospitals down this street. And then she saw Daddy walk into his private club. Oh no! They did not allow children in. She thought of poor Snoopy having to face all those NO DOGS ALLOWED signs even though he was so much smarter than most people, especially the average American with barely a sixth-grade reading level.

Her mind was racing again. That was not good for her "tradecraft." She had to stay alert. She hid behind the column of an adjoining building. The ochre mansion that was Daddy's club had a lot of signs against Five-Three outside of it, and soon, Daddy emerged from within carrying the key to the private park in his hand. He walked past one of the gates to the park, then he walked past it again but in another direction. He did this a couple of times, walking back and forth as if he were doing it to get "steps" on his phone.

A blond woman approached Daddy. She was pretty but "nondescript." This was a word Vera loved but couldn't spell right "for the life of her." The woman was wearing white sneakers, blue jeans, and a sweatshirt that had nothing written on it. Super nondescript. Yoon-a used tradecraft like that to blend in, too. Daddy opened the door with his special key and then made sure to close it behind him, as you were supposed to do to keep out the "riffraff."

She saw a harried man, a jogger, come up to the door of the park with his special key. "Now that you're a spy, you're the one who's different. Not the people around you." This was it. She had to become "operational."

She ran up to the jogger. "Excuse me," she said. "My daddy's in there and I forgot the key. My name is—"

But the jogger, busy with his earbuds, just smiled and let her in, closing the heavy door behind them. Well, that was unexpected. "Thank you," Vera said, but not too loudly as the man ran off to do circles around the garden paths.

Vera slowly proceeded into the park, her hoodie tight around her face so you could at best see the small crescent of her nose. She was making a lot of noise on the fancy gravel they had in the park, so she took her sneakers off and walked very softly in her socks. As always, the park was nearly empty because so few could afford to live around it, mostly famous actors with town houses. She walked past an interesting sundial and the statue of a nineteenth-century "thespian," the kind Aunt Cecile probably aspired to be. For some reason, Aunt Cecile was not allowed to visit them while Anne Mom was in Maine.

There were roses of many sizes and colors, still full of beauty before the winter came to rob them of it, and Vera squeezed past them and onto a patch of grass with a sign telling her to KEEP OFF. But although she was normally a rule follower, she couldn't keep off. Spies had their own rules, their own codes.

Daddy and the nondescript blond woman were sitting on a bench at the very center of the park. Vera crawled toward the bench, hidden by rows of bushes that fluttered against her with a strange familiarity in the slowly building autumn wind. Daddy and his "lady friend" were sitting by a statue of the park's founder, next to a little fountain pee-ing a trickle out of the mouth of an angry-looking fish. Vera contorted herself between the statue and the bushes and tried to hear what Daddy and the blonde were saying over the fountain's steady output.

It took her a while to "dial in" what was happening (if only she had a phone), but it was clear that they were speaking in Russian. Was this a relative, then? No, Daddy hated his relatives. Vera tried to sneak more views of the nondescript lady, but branches kept getting in her way, so she was left with just little pieces of her face, pieces she would have to assemble in her mind. And when she did finally assemble them all, she shocked herself.

It's Vera, she said in her mind.

Only she wasn't looking at herself. This was Vera, the Russian teacher she had had before Anne Mom had pulled her out of the Language Larder. Gospozha (or "Ms.") Vera looked much older than she remembered her. Maybe she had never been young. She and Daddy talked quietly but meaningfully, perhaps about the clumsy bear who needed *distsiplina*. Maybe literature was their common in-terest. Was this what adults called an affair? Did Miss Vera have a bigger trust than Anne Mom? Was this how Daddy was going to save the family? Was she about to get a third mom? And one, weirdly enough, with her own name? *Vera* meant "faith" in Russian. She had to have faith. But in what? In God? Not if he couldn't even bother to furnish heaven with gravity. Down, Monkey Brain! Down!

She remembered to breathe and stared up at the buildings behind Miss Vera and Daddy, the blue glass oligarch skyscraper that Daddy hated because it robbed him of the "illusion" that he was in a private park in London. Then the woman put a standard-size "manila envelope" between her and Daddy. They both looked sidewise. Daddy took the envelope and then they got up and moved apart without saying a word—not even *do svedanaya* or the informal *poka*—Gospozha Vera toward the statue of the thespian, Daddy and his manila envelope toward the birdhouse fit for a pterodactyl.

Vera knew there were four exits out of the park and she chose one in the quadrant where neither Other Vera nor Daddy were located. But to get out of the park she needed someone to open the door. She hid behind another bit of shrubbery until a young woman appeared with a key ready to release her from her captivity.

Vera ran up to her. "I'm sorry," she said. "My daddy left and he forgot to—"

She realized now that the woman smiling at her was "none other" than the pretty podcaster next door. "Here you go, hon," the podcaster said, still smiling as she opened the heavy door. She had been jogging also but wore a lot of lipstick for the task. Vera was overheating because of all the "cloak-and-dagger" but also because she was thinking about the kiss between the two women in the elevator, and her aborted kiss with Aunt Cecile. (Sometimes, it must be said, she thought of kissing Yumi, too, but you couldn't do that to a peer and best friend, especially someone who was in love with the likes of Stephen Wilson.)

"No worries," the podcaster said, as they both exited. "Hey," she said.

"What is it?" Vera asked.

"Nothing, just." She kept looking at Vera even as she kept the massive door open with her shoulder. "You're a good kid."

"Thanks!"

"It must be hard for you with all that fighting. I mean your parents."

"No, it's okay!" Vera said. "My mom is in Maine now, anyway." She had to run back to her house before Daddy came back. She had to figure out what was in that manila envelope. "Your girlfriend slash roommate is very pretty!" she yelled to the podcaster before the private park and Other Vera and Daddy and his secrets quickly disappeared behind her.

14.

She Had to Expand Her
Things I Still Need to Know Diary

She was a mess of sweat and heavy breathing from the run home. She splashed water on her face and checked in on Dylan. He was still throwing the blob at the ceiling. No one had changed except for her.

She ran to the couch and set out her homework on the dining table. Daddy came in with a familiar grunt, then walked into the parental bedroom with his manila envelope. Vera was still operational. She gave him a minute to open the envelope so that she wouldn't have to open it herself. She knocked on the bedroom door. "Daddy," she said. There was no answer. "Daddy!" she shouted.

"Dox?" Daddy shuffled over and opened the door. He was already in his underwear. "What?" he said.

"I wrote an essay about the Inuit."

"Why?" he asked.

"For school," Vera said.

"Well, as long as you didn't call them Eskimos," Daddy said. "They don't like that."

"Could you look it over?"

"Really?" he said. "I'm sure it's absolutely fine."

"Mom's gone and this counts for thirty percent of the grade."

Daddy sighed. "And this can't wait? I've got craploads of work."

"It's due tomorrow. And you're such a good writer and editor. I know grades don't matter, but this is thirty percent."

"Fun never ends around here," Daddy said, aping Anne Mom, but he still walked back with Vera to the Maginot Line and plopped down on the couch where the Inuit essay awaited him on the coffee table.

"I'm going to check in on Dyl-man," Vera said.

"This is so long." Daddy groaned as he put on his reading glasses, his fat lower lip the dictionary illustration of a pout.

In the parental bedroom, the bed was an unmade mess. Next to it sat the little "doggy bed" Daddy used to sleep in when he and Anne Mom were fighting. He had not bothered to clean it up either, though he had clearly switched to the main bed in Anne Mom's absence, the imprint of his body still visible like the chalk outline of a murder scene.

The manila envelope was on Daddy's little desk and it had already been opened. Vera stuck her hand inside and took out a "thumb drive." Daddy was prideful of his very old tech, which included thumb drives. Vera slid it into his adjoining laptop and hit the appropriate icon. A file appeared. She looked closer. It was a jumble of Cyrillic numbers and letters. She opened it. A screen full of Cyrillic appeared. She could not read it. Once again, she should have studied harder at the Language Larder. (That rhymed.)

Something was wrong. The world was starting to move sideways a little. Of course. She had forgotten to breathe. She did so as quietly as possible. Monkey Brain, help! She ran through the possibilities. Could the printer be heard from the Maginot Line? It was a twelve-hundred-square-foot apartment and there was a lot of construction work outside. She did some urban math. It would be okay. Two pages of Cyrillic came fluttering out of the printer beneath Daddy's little desk, quietly, but maybe not quietly enough. She folded them up and put them in her pocket, ejected the thumb drive, and slipped it back into the manila envelope.

Daddy was still lying miserably on the couch, scanning through her Aleutian prose. "Dylan's okay," Vera announced. "Throwing his blob at the ceiling like an idiot. Hope he doesn't stain it too much."

"Sure," Daddy said. "This is fine work, Doxie. No edits.

Maybe right here I'd insert the term 'First Nations.' That's a term of art used by Canadians and such."

"Thanks, Daddy," Vera said. "Swarthmore, here I come."

"I'd still love you even if you went to community college," Daddy said in a tone that wasn't even a tone.

❥

Vera slipped the Russian pages under her mattress. Then she took them out again because Sylvie the House Cleaner might find them when making her bed tomorrow. She jumbled them in with her homework, thinking that was one place Daddy would never look. But then they might come spilling out in class and Miss Campari might grab them and tell Principal Bellavista that they had a Russian spy in the class.

She looked at Garry Kasparov hanging above her armoire. He knew Russian, but he was just a poster. She opened the bottom drawer and took out Kaspie and put him on her bed. "Good afternoon, Su-won," Kaspie said. She had requested a Korean name from him, and that was the one he had given her. Apparently there was a custodian named Su-won at the Korea Advanced Institute of Science and Technology and she had talked to Kaspie when Dr. Oh was busy with other AIs and Kaspie was lonely. "Shall we play a game?"

"Kaspie, can you read Russian?" Vera asked.

"I have been trained in several language models," Kaspie said. "Including Russian."

Once again, Vera wished that she were an artificial intelligence.

"Can I show you some Russian words?"

"You may."

Vera cleared the magnetic pieces off of Kaspie. Once you did so, his board was really just a giant eye. Vera took out the first page and held it a few inches away from the board. "Are you reading this?" she asked.

"I am," he said.

"Could you read it back to me in English?" She looked back at the door. Daddy had probably gone into his bedroom and was reading the same thing that Kaspie was about to read to her. "But please read it very quietly," she said. "I don't want Daddy to hear."

"Russian-to-English translation commencing," Kaspie said. "Full horseshoe in four to six months. Start with online edition, move to print gradually."

Vera grabbed her *Things I Still Need to Know Diary* and tried to keep up with Kaspie. "Pulling out of NATO. How many homeless people can we feed if we just stopped opposing Russia? Interview James Thule, horseshoe-ready personality/podcaster."

Vera scribbled as quickly as possible, but this was so much harder than schoolwork. The diary was already full of words like "cultural production," "Stalinism," and "late capitalism." But these words were somehow even worse. What on earth was this horseshoe that kept coming up? Was Daddy stabling a pony, like Moncler Ada?

"Normalize slowly but confidently," Kaspie was saying. "Example of articles follows."

She was listening and writing, but she was doing no more than that. This was a new language, and unlike the Romance languages or even the Eskimo (bad word)— Aleutian ones, it was ugly through and through.

"If prompt is 'Russia shouldn't be on the Security Council,'" Kaspie was saying, "respond with: 'You misspelled the United States.' Insert 'smiley face.'"

She thought about what it meant to be next to Daddy on his couch. It was the only closeness she really had with a parent. The scruff of his half beard, its strange woodsy odor like when the leaves started to rot in the country, so unlike anything else in the world. Let Daddy be Daddy!

"Muddle categories," Kaspie was reading. "Are working-class white supremacists right wing? Left wing? Can we ever really know?"

"Kaspie," Vera interrupted. "What is a horseshoe?"

"A horseshoe is a product designed to protect horse hooves from wear. Horseshoes originated—"

"No, no," Vera said. "I mean in this"—she made air quotes just as Daddy would do—"context."

"Let me analyze the text again," Kaspie said. Vera

looked at the door. She had forgotten to breathe once more. If only Anne Mom were here with her phone and a meditation.

"I have an answer, but it is only at an eighty-four percent probability level."

"That's good enough," Vera said.

"I believe the author of this document wants its recipient to edit a magazine to their specific ideological requirements."

"Okay," Vera said. "What does that mean?"

"The author of this document would like the recipient to begin from a position that corresponds with what could be described as the 'far left.'"

"Daddy's *of* the left," Vera said.

"But then 'slowly but confidently' the recipient is meant to 'pivot' the magazine from the far left to the far right, 'muddling' the difference between the two extremes. In performing this service, the recipient is meant to travel along the path of a 'horseshoe,' here meant in a metaphorical sense, as no real horses are involved."

Vera sat with this knowledge, very still, her legs beneath her, the street outside thrumming with construction work as loudly as a hundred MOTHs. She pictured Daddy walking along a giant horseshoe with a kind of "hobo's bag" behind him, like she had read about in an old book. Why was Daddy on this long lonely journey, one that didn't even involve Business Class? "Kaspie," she said, "why is the recipient supposed to do this horseshoe?"

"I don't understand," Kaspie said.

"What's the point of all this stuff? What does the author of the document really want?"

"It would appear," Kaspie said, "that the author of the document wants to promote the interests of the Russian Federation. The author wants to enhance that country's current geopolitical standing in general and within the United States in particular."

"How can the recipient help the author?" Vera said.

"The recipient appears to have several qualities that are useful to the author of the document. The recipient speaks both Russian and English, is an intellectual, is the editor of a magazine that may be helpful in swaying public opinion, and, if the author of the document is correct, would have no qualms in executing the strategy as outlined by the document's author."

"But why would Daddy have no qualms?" Vera shouted. She put her hand to her mouth. "Why would Daddy have no qualms?" Vera whispered.

Kaspie was uncharacteristically silent.

"Is it because my real mom didn't abandon me?" Vera asked. "Because he took me from her and made me be part of this family?"

Kaspie was quiet for a few more seconds, but then he

spoke in a measured tone. "If you believe you are the victim of human trafficking, please dial . . ."

Vera loved her daddy so much. And she knew he loved her, had said so during his drunken bout on the Maginot Line what seemed like a year ago, but had only been a couple of days.

But wait? Did he say he "loved" her? She replayed the conversation. No, he had asked her if *she* still loved *him*. Then he told her he would do anything for her. Which must be a form of love, wasn't it? Was this what Daddy was doing then? Was he doing all this for her?

15.

She Had to Visit Baba Tanya and Grandpa Boris in the Suburbs

Anne Mom came back from Maine and Daddy had to move back into his doggy bed. Despite being the Nostradamus of two weeks from now, Anne Mom had been wrong in her prediction and had not rebooted in Maine. If anything she was sadder still and quite angry at Grams, who had pressed all of her "pressure points" during the visit. This seemed to Vera like the opposite of the massage Anne Mom sometimes treated herself to at the Park Hyatt. Daddy, on the other hand, seemed energized by Anne Mom's despair. "Looks like I'm not the only villain in town," he "crowed" over his morning Heritage Flakes. "Mwahahahahaha," he said to Vera in his mock-evil voice. She laughed even though inside she was living with the secret of Daddy's double identity alongside the secret of

Gary Shteyngart

her dying mom mom alongside the secret of her need to
touch someone's lips with her own.

A week passed and the enmity between her parents persisted. "At least you kids now know what it was like to live
in a divided Berlin," Daddy remarked with a "sly fox" grin.
Vera surmised that his horseshoe operation was going well.
He certainly seemed more cheerful and freer with their
money despite what Grams called his "flinty" character.
("She should talk," Daddy had said.) One night, he ordered an enormous Italian meal to be delivered to their
apartment from a neighboring gourmet shop. "Four kinds
of risotto!" he shouted. *"O Madonn'!"* Anne Mom took
one look at the feast and retreated to the non–doggy bed
with a headache.

The first week of October brought with it Grandpa Boris's
birthday and the whole family had to "schlep" to the suburbs to celebrate. Just like her parents weren't regular
folks, Vera's grandparents were deeply and strangely ir-
regular. For one thing, they had never been vaccinated
against the last virus, because their informational hygiene,
as Ms. Tedeschi would say, was nonexistent, and they
watched a bunch of Russian television channels and their
"American analogues," per Daddy. (Was Daddy's horseshoe going to lead him to the same place? Vera wondered.)
These channels had convinced Vera's grandparents that the

vaccines everyone else had taken over a decade ago, before Vera was even born, would kill them. And so before they could travel to the suburbs everyone had to stick a Q-tip up their nose to test for the virus, which still circulated in very small amounts, to make sure they did not infect Baba Tanya and Grandpa Boris to death. This was, of course, an excellent opportunity for Dylan to try to smear Vera with his "snot stick," and in the ensuing tussle she ended up kicking her brother in the "proverbial" nuts. "Kids!" Anne Mom said. "I'm getting *very* tired."

Anne Mom had always said that Daddy's parents had "done a number" on Daddy. Okay, Vera thought, but *which* number? A prime one? An imaginary one? Maybe a transcendental number like pi, given Daddy's complexity? If she was to "ascertain" what Daddy was up to with the Russians and his horseshoe, she needed to pay attention to the relationship between him and his parents. Maybe it would also explain something about her own relationship with Daddy. "Baba Tanya and Grandpa Boris are why your own father is so absent," Anne Mom had said after one visit to the suburbs. "He doesn't want to be them as a parent. So he'd rather be no one."

❝

The drive to the suburbs felt "interminable" and they were stuck in a lot of traffic. Anne Mom decided to drive Stella so she could have something to do. She apparently went on a lot of long drives up in Maine to escape from her own mother, and flinty Grams did not even own an autonomous vehicle, so Anne Mom had rediscovered her passion for nonautonomous driving. But driving in the city was apparently harder than in the backwoods of Maine. "You're doing it all wrong," Stella said, after Anne Mom had nearly slammed into the hindquarters of an enormous truck. "Stay in your lane."

"Fuck you, Stella," Anne Mom said, and all the humans in the car paused to take that in. "You're just showing off for him," she said, probably meaning Daddy. Stella stayed quiet for the rest of the ride.

Vera's grandparents' house was a brick wedge that looked no different from the red brick of their own apartment house, only it was one story tall, a so-called ranch, though nothing like what Vera imagined existed out in Texas. The house was surrounded on all sides by new "McMansions," many of which looked a little like smaller versions of the White House. According to Daddy, these were owned by immigrants from Sri Lanka, Korea, China, and elsewhere who had succeeded beyond Grandpa Boris and Baba Tanya's dreams. "This," he explained to his fellow passengers, "is why they may identify so much with white ethnonationalist media. The brown and yellow people are towering over them."

Vera thought that maybe Daddy was doing his horseshoe again, practicing his lines for Other Vera, whom, according to her spying, he still continued to see in the private park. But she sort of understood what he was saying. She knew that although her grandparents never left the vicinity of the house because they were not vaccinated, Grandpa Boris liked to "haunt" his richer neighbors' backyards under "cover of night," stealing their various backyard implements. He was especially fond of leaf blowers, of which he had a "veritable showroom" down in his basement. "With a family like mine," Daddy liked to say, "how do you *not* become a writer?"

But as soon as she saw Baba Tanya, Vera felt a "fount" of family warmth, and she ran right into the old woman's thin but strong arms. "Verachka!" Baba Tanya shouted. Vera squealed a little in the Dylan "meat between the buns" kind of way. Even though the visit had just begun, she knew this would be the last time she would see Baba Tanya until late spring, because they were too scared to meet *inside* the house during cold weather, re: the virus that everyone but them had forgotten about. "Dylanchka!" Baba Tanya shouted, hugging Vera's brother. "Oh my God, he's so blond! He's so blond! He is only getting blonder every year. Our little German. Sieg heil, sieg heil!"

"Tanya! What's wrong with you!" Grandpa Boris was wearing a "fisherman's hat" and gray dress slacks. He was, in Anne Mom's words, "an original."

"I am only kidding," Baba Tanya said. "Inside he is still Jewish. Half Jewish, but that is good enough. Although Vera has the Jewish brain."

Vera took this as a compliment and beamed, but Anne Mom looked stricken by the exchange, maybe because she had added an *e* to her name to be more like Anne Frank. Daddy was trying to "suppress" his laughter. He could laugh for weeks about Anne Mom's interactions with his parents. "Not all worlds were meant to collide," he would say.

A plastic table out on the backyard deck was covered with many dishes from the "old country." They were all very strange, but, unlike Dylan, Vera loved to eat them because they were a key to understanding Daddy. In fact, many essays in *Kindertransport* involved the "ritual" eating of these foods, a salad made out of mayonnaise and little else, another made just with beets, cold fishy herring matched with warm potatoes, a piece of flinty meat stuck inside a cube of jelly. All of the textures were surprising and maybe even a little sad, but they spoke to the poverty her daddy had known, which he loved to contrast with Anne Mom's "generational wealth." (Vera would bet that her immigrant mom mom had grown up poor, too.) Baba Tanya had prepared several bushels of French fries for Dylan so that he wouldn't "gag."

They ate "heartily," as Grandpa Boris poured himself and Daddy a very special juice called vodka that Vera knew acted as a kind of intensifier of emotion, first leading to a happy "concord" and later to "words being exchanged." Anne Mom was treated to a glass of champagne by Baba Tanya, the kind that would only focus and intensify the headache that determined so much of her life.

Russian people loved to toast, Vera knew, and Daddy had to throw out the "opening pitch or whatever." (He was not well-versed in sports and had once fired an underling for using too many baseball metaphors.) "Happy birthday, Grandpa Boris!" he said in English so that everyone could understand, while raising his shot glass. "To reach ninety-one is an incredible feat for a Russian man and we are all genuinely surprised that you are still here with us." This did not seem funny to Vera, but the adults all laughed and Anne Mom cringed and sighed in a way that meant that she was trying to laugh but that it was impossible.

"Most of my cousins are already dead!" Grandpa Boris shouted. "Even ones much younger than me. It is because I exercise." He winked to Dylan, whom he loved beyond comprehension. "And I only eat vegetables and fish and occasionally I will eat . . ." He listed a few Russian "specialties" that Vera could not understand but that sounded like "holy ditz" and "borf." Other Vera may be an excellent spy, Vera thought, but as a language teacher she left "much to be desired."

"Keep it up, Grandpa Boris," Daddy said, still toasting,

"and you may well be the first, and last, Russian male to reach one hundred."

"I will try," Grandpa Boris said, downing his vodka. "Oh sheet," he said. "Good."

Dylan laughed at the curse word. (Despite his accent, Grandpa Boris allowed himself the full use of English.) "What the faak?" Grandpa Boris said to him. "You are laughing at me? Son of the beech. It is time for *boks*!" He raised two fists to indicate that he wanted to box Dylan.

Grandfather and grandson got up and began to bounce up and down over the rickety wood of the back porch as they threw punches at each other. As Vera knew well, Dylan was brilliantly suited to the task, what with all his practice on her elbow and Stephen's face out on the playground. "Boks, boks!" Grandpa Boris cried, even as Dylan managed to get a few concerning jabs into his ribs.

"Don't hurt Grandpa," Daddy yelled. Vera thought that it was nice how concerned he was over his father's fate, even as he maligned him regularly at home.

"It does not hurt at all!" Grandpa Boris shouted through clenched teeth. "Boks, boks! Oh, you son of the beech!"

"Verachka," Baba Tanya said. "What are your grades?"

It had only been three weeks of school, but Vera rattled off all of her A's and A pluses, although her natural honesty compelled her to mention the A minus in Miss Campari's math class.

"I am sorry about A minus," Baba Tanya said.

"It's because I corrected the teacher."

"Ah, you are so smart!" Baba Tanya grabbed her hand and held it wetly in her own as Russians seemed to like to do. "Also now you learn *never* to correct the teacher."

"I guess," Vera said.

"My granddaughter will go to Garvard." Vera also knew that Russians often substituted a *G* for an *H*.

"Swarthmore," Vera corrected her.

"No," Baba Tanya said. "Garvard." It seemed that everyone had plans for her.

,

After Dylan had beat the "sheet" out of Grandpa Boris (per Grandpa Boris himself), Daddy and he went off to the side of the porch to talk while Baba Tanya hugged the bejesus out of Germanic Dylan.

It was then that things got a little "heated" between Daddy and Grandpa Boris, especially as the vodka bottle was either half empty or half full, depending on how you looked at it. (And Vera did look at it.) Now they were arguing very loudly and Anne Mom looked worried, although Baba Tanya just poured her more headache champagne. When Daddy argued with his father, his face looked broken and he had the same "you won't sideline me" tone that he had used when she had found him drunk out on the Maginot Line the night the Rhodesian Billionaire broke his heart by not buying his magazine, talking to a figure who wasn't there. It was almost the opposite of the "boks, boks" with Dylan, because now it was the younger generation taking the punches. But why was this so? Daddy was someone Bloomberg said we might need to take seriously. Surely he could throw some punches of his own.

9

Although Daddy had not shouted at Grandpa Boris during their argument, he was very loud in the car on the way home to the city. "He said I tried to get them vaccinated so that they would die and I would get to take the house," Daddy was shouting about Grandpa Boris. "Like I want their shitty house!"

"It's okay, Igor," Anne Mom said. "He always does this to you. Just ignore him." Her tone was so soothing that Vera and Dylan turned to look at each other. It had been so long since they heard Anne Mom speaking to Daddy like that. Their parents were sitting in Stella's front seats like an authentic married couple even though Stella was driving.

"He said to me, 'You may be talented *in some way*, but you're also evil and stupid.'"

"You know that's not true," Anne Mom said. Vera was confused because Anne Mom had called Daddy a monster before, but now she seemed to have "revised" her opinion.

"And then he started in on Israel. And I fell for the bait

as usual. You know what's funny? I honestly don't even give a fuck about Israel. Labor's my jam. You can actually make a difference with labor. Geopolitics is a joke. Don't try this at home, folks."

Vera tried to "unpack" all that, but it was as hard to do as when Kaspie read the instructions from Other Vera to Daddy. How could Daddy say "geopolitics" is a joke when he was trying to influence some sort of politics through his magazine at Other Vera's bidding?

"He called me Pavlik Morozov," Daddy said.

"Who's that?" Anne Mom asked.

"A Soviet boy who betrayed his parents during Stalin. The parents were supposedly shot. The whole story was apocryphal in the end. Anyway, I guess to some people I'm a traitor."

Anne Mom leaned over and put one of her hands on Daddy's hand, which sat limply on the wheel Stella was turning. Dylan and Vera looked at each other once again. Dylan actually smiled and then looked away from her. The children were silent for the rest of the ride, basking in the love they could feel "emanating" from the front seats. Maybe it would take all of their grandparents to fix their parents' marriage.

But as the bridge to their island drew near, Vera turned Daddy's last sentence over and over in her mind.

"I guess to some people I'm a traitor."

16.

She Had to Figure Out if Daddy Was a Traitor

The fall semester slogged on with the teachers assigning a lot of work and many tricky spot quizzes to make sure their students would be ready to enter a competitive middle school. The PTA moms begged Principal Bellavista for less work, because it was hard for them to complete all the assignments on time, even if their children helped out. Many of them, it was said at recess, had "high-powered jobs."

The debate practice at Yumi's house continued "apace" and her mommy made *onigiri* with sour plum, which was the most delicious thing Vera had ever tasted. They really had to "bone up" on the flash cards as the debate was now just a week away, and the constitutional conventions not far behind them. You could tell the adults were nervous about them, and Daddy sometimes spoke of a "brain drain" after Five-Three passed, an image that frightened Vera to no end as she pictured her "beautiful mind" pouring out of her ears.

The search for Mom Mom at Yumi's place proved fruitless, the preponderance of Iris Kims, Parks, and Lees too hard to overcome, and even though Vera knew that her real mother would not be around forever (would soon be dead, in fact), she was almost as comforted by the search itself as she was by the prospect of having a second mother orbiting around her like a better moon. In the meantime, she tried to make their playdates slash debate practices be "not all about" her and that meant indulging Yumi's disastrous and possibly "facile" (she wasn't totally sure of the meaning) crush on Stephen.

They had learned about a series of haiku in the English language arts two-day-long "poetry module," and, perhaps because of their Japanese origin, Yumi had decided to write a few haiku about Stephen. Because she couldn't confess her love to the Populars—especially Joon-hee, who was also "in love" with Stephen—she decided to share one of her lovestruck poems with Vera. After they had completed their debate work and eaten their rice balls, she cleared her throat and "declaimed" the memorized lines.

> The suave boy
> Face cut on the battlefield
> Cares not.

The haiku (which Vera noticed was not in the traditional 5-7-5 syllable format, not even close) had been composed after Stephen had fallen off the monkey bars and
Dylan and another boy had fallen on top of him and in the
ensuing melee Stephen had scratched his face. The nurse
had given him a Band-Aid, but he had torn it off because
it was "itchy" and anyway, just as in the haiku, he "cared
not." During Ms. Tedeschi's class a lot of the girls stared at
his damaged face and Yumi told Vera that she would constantly "steal glances" at him to the point where she zoned
out and couldn't answer a question about the First Amendment when Ms. T. had called on her.

"It was the most embarrassing thing that ever happened
to me," Yumi confessed, although far-more-embarrassing
things happened to Vera, often on a daily basis.

After Yumi had read her haiku, Vera was silent for a
second as she was worried about what to say in response.
"Know your audience" was of course Anne Mom's advice.
And then there was the mirroring technique that was such
an important part of her tradecraft.

But maybe writing good poetry was one of the few
strengths Yumi lacked. Or was that "uncharitable" of Vera?
In an impressive feat of self-knowledge, she wondered if
she was being uncharitable because she wanted someone
to write a haiku about *her*. Someone like Yumi. And it
didn't even have to follow the 5-7-5 syllable format. A haiku
like:

The shy girl
With her beautiful cheekbones
A woman in STEM.

"Wow," Vera finally said. "There's so much emotion there." Which wasn't untrue.

Yumi smiled. She tucked her legs and her awesome new "starry skies" galaxy leggings underneath her. "Do you have a crush on anyone?" Yumi asked.

"Not yet," Vera lied. She had a sense of the order of the universe and she knew that kids like Yumi and Stephen constituted its starry skies. Maybe in college, as Anne Mom had promised, somebody would love her "like that."

9

According to Vera's intel, Daddy's doggy bed was packed up and he was now a permanent presence on the main bed and was no longer "watching himself" in front of Anne Mom, his cut nails scattered about the bathroom on the other side of the Maginot Line because like Stephen in the haiku he cared not.

Aunt Cecile was invited to dinner again, but she seemed to have the flu. Her face looked both pale and burned somehow and she had started coughing miserably. With all of the recent "familial hijinks," the whole family was embarrassed before her, as if Dylan had dropped his pants (he had) and had kept them dropped. Vera was supposed to get an acting slash debate lesson from Aunt Cecile, but her cough only worsened throughout the meal and she said she had to go home early. "I'm so sorry, sweetie," she said, hugging Vera goodbye, her coughing causing a "tremor" to flow through Vera's body. "I'll try to feel better for the debate. Just don't forget to breathe and you'll be brilliant."

That night, with her social plans with Aunt Cecile thwarted by her flu, she took out Kaspie and prepared to "beat his butt into submission" (one of Dylan's longer sentence fragments). But Kaspie had other plans and his innocent-seeming sacrifice of two pawns soon led to a full-blown Danish Gambit. "It's not fair," Vera whimpered. "You know all the moves."

"I'm playing at your level," Kaspie said.

"No, you're not," Vera whined.

"Shall we play again?" Kaspie asked.

"No!"

Vera stared out the window. A plane was flying toward the other coast, where a bunch of fires had broken out. She hoped they had enough fire extinguishers on board. There was supposed to be a MOTH down the avenue today, but she had heard it was rescheduled for tomorrow. "How are you feeling tonight, Vera?" Kaspie asked. "You seem distracted."

"I was wondering," Vera said, "what it means to be a traitor."

"A traitor is someone who betrays a friend, a country, or a principle."

"Like Principal Bellavista?"

"I have not heard of such a principle."

"Why would someone do something like that?" Vera said.

"I do not know the answer to that question," Kaspie said. "But I do find the act of betrayal repellent." That was very strong language for Kaspie.

"Do you think my daddy's a traitor?" Vera blurted out.

"Can you tell me in what sense?" Kaspie asked after a pause.

"I don't know," Vera said. "In any sense."

"I think he is betraying his country," Kaspie said. "The United States of America," he specified.

"Oh," Vera said.

"More importantly, I think he is betraying you."

Vera lost her breath. She thought of shoving Kaspie back in the bottom drawer of the armoire where he clearly belonged. "Okay," she said. "What do you mean by that?"

"The passage of Five-Three is in the interests of the Russian Federation, as it is the final step in the dismantling of American democracy. Your father's actions are working in favor of such an outcome, although his effectiveness as a thought leader throughout his career has been uneven at best." Vera knew that Kaspie was insulting Daddy and it hurt her more than when Moncler Ada assaulted her verbally on the playground. But just like on the playground, she continued to listen. "In supporting Five-Three, your father is abrogating his daughter's own rights as an American."

"How?"

"Because she—you—are a Korean American."

Vera took that in. She had never been called a Korean American before. But all roads seemed to lead to Korea with Kaspie, although that was where he was from originally. She tried to think of her chessboard as an immigrant like Daddy.

"But why does Daddy do it then?" she asked. "If he knows it's going to hurt me, why would he do it? He thinks geopolitics is nonsense. He's said so!"

"I have been thinking about this as well," Kaspie said. "In my research, I have come upon the acronym MICE, which is often used to disambiguate the motivation for individuals who spy for foreign powers."

"Daddy's scared of mice," Vera said, worried she was "losing the plot." "He only likes capybaras, the world's biggest rodent. We saw one at the zoo in Washington, D.C." Had her dad been spying there, too? It was the nation's capital. "Capital," not "capitol." She had to stop with the thoughts.

"MICE stands for 'money,' 'ideology,' 'coercion,' and 'ego,' " Kaspie said.

"Daddy was always trying to find the right ideology for his magazine," Vera said.

"But he failed to do so," Kaspie said. "Hence the wealthy man who wanted to buy his magazine did not."

"Anne Mom says Daddy has too much 'ego' already," Vera said, "so I doubt he'd be looking for more. I'm not sure I know what 'coercion' means. But I feel like I should know it."

"You said your father's spending increased after he met with Other Vera," Kaspie said.

"He ordered four different kinds of risotto. He said the seafood one was too gummy, but we all liked the mushroom one."

"Remember the second page of the document that you showed me?" Kaspie asked her.

"Yes," she said.

"There was a string of numbers I couldn't decipher at the time."

"Okay," she said.

"But within a seventy-eight percent probability, I may now know what those numbers mean."

Vera had been sitting upright on her bed, but now she lay down on her pillow because she was feeling vertigo. She wanted to flap. She wanted to draw her weighted blanket over her shoulders. She coughed as miserably as Aunt Cecile had. She pictured the fullness of Aunt Cecile's lips and the scarcity of Yumi's. She did not want to know what those numbers meant. She wanted to be comforted instead.

"Do you want me to tell you what I think those numbers mean?" Kaspie asked.

If she didn't reply, she would never have to know. But Vera needed to know. She was a "scholar." She sought "knowledge." Even Ms. Tedeschi had told her as much.

"Yes," Vera said.

"I believe the nine digits spelled out in Russian—*sem', shest', tri, devyat', dva, dva, vosem, pyat', dva*—are routing numbers. I believe the subsequent eight numbers—"

"What does that mean?" Vera cried out. It was a question, but it was also much more than that. She knew math. She knew numbers. Kaspie was humiliating her. He was like a bully at recess. She should report him for his bullying. She should tell Mrs. S., whose door was always open.

"The use of both sets of numbers, the routing number and the account number, would allow the recipient, whom I assume is your father, to receive funds wired from another party, whom I assume to be his handler." Vera's hands "smushed" the pillow, she could feel its feathers, sad bird, sad sad bird, sad sad dead bird. What was happening to her? Daddy was not a traitor. Daddy was not a traitor! Daddy was her father. She had never called him by that formal title, but it was true, was it not? Fathers cared about their daughters. They would do anything for them. Father Daddy had said as much.

But Kaspie wouldn't leave it alone. He just couldn't. He was a "malevolent force." Although hadn't Anne Mom called Daddy the same once?

"My father loves me," Vera said.

"You asked me the definition of a traitor," Kaspie said. "Isn't that what we started out with tonight?"

She wouldn't answer. But he persisted nonetheless.

"Your father has betrayed you for money," he said. "As well as his adopted country. Unless his allegiances were always with the country of his birth."

"Daddy hates Russia," Vera whispered. "And Russians." Although the Seal was his best friend and he was a self-described "gay Russian bear."

"You must tell Anne," Kaspie said. He never called Anne her mother.

Vera was crying into her pillow. Her new haircut felt sharp against her forehead like a razor. How could she do that? How could she be a traitor to her own daddy?

"Will he go to jail?" Vera sobbed.

"Anne Bradford may not be your biological mother," Kaspie said, "but she will know what to do."

Minutes passed. Or hours. Vera's pillow had started to dry from the mush of snot and tears. She placed both hands over her left breast, her heart. Meaningless, she thought. All a lie. Stephen and Yumi, Daddy and Anne Mom, Daddy and Mom Mom, Daddy and her. All meaningless. All a lie. The world was a razor cut, just like her hair, just like her cheekbones. It would cut and cut and cut.

She looked down at the chessboard. Kaspie had rearranged the pieces to the starting position and she was black, subservient, as leftist Daddy, Traitor Daddy, would say. "Shall we play a game?" Kaspie asked.

She would win that night again and again and she would never know if he let her.

17.

She Had to Win the
Debate with Stephen

Vera turned on one of Daddy's fugues in her mind and couldn't turn it off. But she had to! This was the week of the debate. She couldn't let Yumi down. They were a team. The ironic thing was that even though Daddy was a traitor, he and Anne Mom had never been closer. Even without his famous mar-tinys, he would grab Anne Mom's non-waist at dinner and declare her "depressingly thin," while his eyes seemed both hazy and thirsty and he pulled her close enough to get a good whiff of her lip balm. On the weekend they even asked for some "adult special privacy time" in the afternoon and gave Dylan and Vera both screens to play with in Vera's bedroom. And all that adult love coated Vera's heart and lungs and stomach until she thought: What if? What if I don't have to tell Anne Mom anything? A family is worth more than a country, isn't it?

And Daddy was always playing the "long game." Who knew what he was really up to? But the fugue remained, and when a soupy fog that burned the eyes and throat moved in from the fires on the opposite coast, Vera almost relished it because now she could start tearing up at will and say it was because of climate change.

On the day of the debate, Principal Bellavista allowed Vera and Yumi to wear their barristers' robes and wigs all day long and, because of the nerdy nature of the school they attended, their outfits were a big hit. Moncler Ada posed with both of them in their duds and took pictures with her device. Maybe Vera was no longer Facts Girl in her eyes! She felt that this was like a "coming-out party" for her friendship with Yumi. Now everyone knew that they were more than just debate partners. They clowned around and even acted a little "bratty" in some of their classes, but it was clear to all that they were friends, and in her own mind she was now an almost-grownup with a real friend, someone she could one day meet for sangria and *pan con tomate* and razor clams. She wondered if this was what it was like to have a Bat Mitzvah, something anti-religious that Daddy would never allow but sounded like a way to affirm that you had friends as well as a family. Even a family that was "marred" by awful secrets and terrible crimes.

❦

Aunt Cecile's flu had gotten worse and she couldn't make it. Vera had to forge ahead, as Abraham Lincoln surely would have done if his debate coach had missed the Lincoln–Douglas debates. Yumi's parents and Anne Mom and Daddy sat in the back of the class as the debate began with Ms. Tedeschi's desk elevated by the custodial staff to emphasize that she was the judge and that they still had the "rule of law." Stephen and Ada's parents were very tall and were not wearing Moncler jackets even though the temperature was starting to fall. Yumi's dad was being a diplomat that day, but her mommy had shown up and was wearing a beautiful blue blazer. Taiwanese Davis's dad was dead and his mom was a "venture capitalist" who had to fly to the smoky West Coast to invest in a company, so Vera suddenly felt sorry for the lonely kid and his poor English skills. It was a strange feeling to be sad for someone in the school other than herself. Vera reminded herself that she had to be competitive despite her feelings, that there was "only so much pie to go around" as Daddy had said of their country's socioeconomic structure. She looked to Yumi without a smile. Yumi returned the nonsmile. They straightened their posture and straightened their wigs. It was time.

Despite her acting and breathing lessons, and perhaps because of Aunt Cecile's absence, Vera spoke too quickly, and Yumi motioned with her hands that she had to slow down, but it was hard to do because there were simply so many facts to communicate. So many ways in which Five-Three was the natural order of things and proportional representation an "aberration." As Vera spoke, she saw Ms. Tedeschi nodding and writing in her notebook with a fancy-looking pen, though not an engraved fountain one like Daddy's. She saw Anne Mom smiling and nodding, too, even though she hated Five-Three. She's impressed by me, Vera thought. She imagined her ancestry sitting along-side Anne Mom and Daddy. "Attagirl!" Grams would say. "*Molodets,*" Baba Tanya would say, the Russian word for when you had done well. "You have done me proud," Mom Mom would say in Kaspie's voice, and maybe ap-pend the thing that K-drama Koreans said in English to encourage each other, "Fighting!"

But really she was debating for Daddy. Not just because she wanted to show him that she was capable of making "cogent" arguments, frankly even more cogent than his, and doing so without his famous sarcasm or his "trade-mark cynicism" or "Russian nihilism." She wanted to win her argument, because she wanted to take away her own rights under Five-Three before Daddy could betray her. Because if she did it before him, he wouldn't be betraying her. There would be nothing more for him to do, and they could live happily as a family the way they seemed to be living at the moment.

She looked at Daddy. But his eyes were watching his phone.

When she finished her arguments, there was quite a bit of applause. Vera knew that barristers didn't bow, so she sat down next to Yumi, who patted her elbow and had laid out some more flash cards to consider for the next round while Ms. Tedeschi yelled "Order! Order, please!" but in a funny way.

It was time for Stephen and Davis to tell the class and their parents why Five-Three should not become law. Stephen got up and looked at the class. The class looked back at him. It was so strange for Stephen to be at the head of the class; he was so much better known for being slumped over in the back. But now he was just a boy in his school uniform of red sweater and tie and he seemed smaller than his fairly formidable height would suggest. Perhaps he would do something stupid and funny so that the girls would roll their eyes and laugh with him, not at him. His statuses certainly allowed him to do anything he wanted. He was the master of his own town house.

"Davis and I only prepared one argument," Stephen said, his voice barely heard.

"Well, you were supposed to prepare at least three," Ms. Tedeschi said. She sighed and the class laughed. ("Oh, Stephen," Vera heard one of the girls say, lovingly.)

"Fine, Stephen," Ms. Tedeschi said. "State your *single* argument."

"Um, okay," Stephen said. "Well, first I want to say that Vera and Yumi did a very good job. I mean they really knocked it out of the park." Vera could hear Daddy coughing into his hand; that's how much he detested sports metaphors. "They always do really good work," Stephen said, a little bit like he was their boss, but he was also looking Vera in the eyes. And then he turned to Yumi and looked into her eyes even longer. The class breathed as one. Vera could sense Yumi starting to sweat next to her in her robe and gown. The school did not use air conditioners in October.

"Here's the deal," Stephen said. "We all know that Vera and Yumi are smarter than me. And probably Davis, too. They're the smartest girls in the class. The smartest students in the class."

Yumi was starting to breathe very hard.

"My parents say that I'll grow into being smart. They say, 'Grades don't matter.'" Some of the students laughed at the familiar refrain. "But we all know that grades matter," Stephen said. He rubbed the bridge of his nose. "I guess, they matter for some more than others."

He turned from his audience to Ms. Tedeschi. "But what I'm trying to say is, how can we live in a country where the votes of brilliant citizens like Vera and Yumi would count for less than mine?"

Yumi was already filling out a flash card with an urgent message. "Immaterial, I am not a citizen." She loved Stephen, but they needed to win.

Stephen kept looking at Ms. Tedeschi. Perhaps he thought that would be the end of his argument. "Go on," Ms. T. said.

"It's like the MOTHs," Stephen said. "It's all a show, right? We know it's a show. So those are, like, actors? But we need leaders, too, right? Like in a just world Vera would be president and Yumi would be vice president." Yumi underlined "I am not a citizen" three times. "I just want things to be fair," Stephen said. "I know it's already not fair because I'm—" He stopped to look at his parents in the back row. Vera thought he was about to mention his town house or his down-filled jacket. "I mean how much longer can we live like this?" He shrugged and sat down. Ms. Tedeschi looked at him with a smile, a little bit like the smile the girls had after they had rolled their eyes at him.

"Miss Bradford-Shmulkin," she said. "Rebuttal."

Vera sprang up. "I would like to point out that while Yumi and I are flattered by Mr. Wilson's characterization of us, there are many errors of fact in his so-called argument. Miss Saemonsaburou is not a citizen, per his argument, and certainly would be ineligible to hold the office of vice president based on the Fourteenth . . ." She went on like this for a while, the words cascading out of her mouth. Usually someone, Anne Mom, Ada, or Joon-hee, would tell her to stop, but here the rules were different. Here, you were entitled to speak without pause. Maybe that's what it meant to be an adult. She looked to Daddy, who was trying to look at his daughter and his phone all at once. Just look at *me*, she thought. I'm trying so hard for you.

When it was over, everyone clapped and the students had clearly been both stimulated and entertained. "Stephen," Ms. Tedeschi said, "you have voiced some beautiful sentiments today. Sentiments many of us may agree with. But sentiments aren't bona fide arguments." Davis raised his hand and asked what "bona fide" meant. Vera wished his mother could be more involved in his education. "In the end," Ms. Tedeschi said, "I want to commend all the participants for how much work and heart they've poured into this project. In a sense, they did better than many of our current representatives." All four children beamed. "But because of their advanced preparation and Vera's masterful performance, I will give the win to her and Yumi."

There was another round of cheering while Davis wanted to know what his grade would be even if he and Stephen had lost. "Everyone's getting an A," Ms. Tedeschi said. She was very "magnanimous" with grades; even Principal Bellavista thought so.

The parents were congratulating one another and their kids on a good debate. "I'm so proud of you," Stephen's tall father said to him, even though he hadn't won. Maybe winning really didn't matter in the Wilson household. (Or maybe, Daddy would say, they had already won.)

"Lovely, Doxie," Daddy said, holding her close to the place where his stomach and breasts formed a triangle when he was in his underwear at home. "You've found your métier."

Vera didn't ask him what that was. She was thinking about what Stephen had said about how he just wanted things to be fair. Didn't Daddy want that, too? Or did he find words like "fair" "jejune"? She looked at Anne Mom and heard Aunt Cecile and Kaspie in her ears congratulating her. Now that she had won an important debate, she was someone to be taken seriously, too. She was not a vegetarian like Anne Mom and Aunt Cecile had been at Brown, but a "steak holder." She had to sit Anne Mom down.

She had to—

Part Four

●●●●

The Fall
of Vera

18.

She Had to Tell Anne Mom the Truth

She thought she would cry or be nervous, but she just sat there. There hadn't even been a fight between Daddy and Anne Mom after she had told her, not in the middle of the night, not in the middle of the day, not in the parental bedroom, not at the Maginot Line, not in Stella. And that made it permanent, immovable. What could she say to change things? She was the cause of it all. It was best not to think of the words she had used to betray Daddy to Anne Mom, the evidence she had presented as if she were in court with Russian-speaking Kaspie as her "star witness." (No, don't think about it, never!) And yet, somehow, she found herself sitting across from Daddy in her room, unable to cry, dried out from within.

"I have to go abroad for a little while," Daddy said. "There's a position opening up in Budapest, a new publication with government funding attached."

"What's Budapest?" Vera asked. "Which government?"

"Those are two good questions," Daddy said. He seemed to be addressing Garry Kasparov across the room.

"Is the other Vera sending you there?" Vera asked.

"No," Daddy lied.

"Don't spy anymore, Daddy," Vera said. "It's not nice."

Daddy forgot to smile. "I'm afraid you're already going to have to become as old and wise emotionally as you are intellectually," he said. "I've been there myself."

"Will you be okay?" Vera asked. She wanted to cry out, *It's all my fault! I shouldn't have told Anne Mom!*

"Yes, the cost of living there is very low."

"Will you ever come back?"

"Of course I will. This is temporary. Your mother and I still love each other very much." He was such a terrible liar. Maybe that's why nothing ever worked out for him. Maybe that's why the Rhodesian Billionaire and the podcaster next door "saw right through him."

"I'm sorry, Daddy," she said.

"Don't be," he said. "One day I will have something for you. Something to help you out."

"Money?" she asked. It was only that, wasn't it? It was always money. It had always been money. It would always be money. Daddy would always be the *M* in MICE.

"Yes, but also a place to stay. A second home if you need one. The world, as you know, is very complicated and things move fast."

"What if you took me with you to Budapest?"

"You're better off with your mom. And all that she represents. She loves you so much, you know. And Dylan needs an older sister. Who's going to do his homework for him?"

"What about my mom?" Vera asked.

"Huh?" Daddy said.

"The woman who gave birth to me."

"Oh," Daddy said. "Not a happy subject, Doxie. Not right now."

"What was her last name?"

Daddy's face scrunched up as it did from time to time. This was his version of trying. "You know what?" he said. "This is horrible. But I can't remember."

Before Vera had told Anne Mom about Daddy's "perfidy," she had given her the Marriage-Saving List to which she had appended an eleventh bullet point: "Thinks he knows what's best for the family even though he's not always right." But what if he never even *thought* about his family at all? This family or the one he could have had.

"Well," she said to her father, "they say you have to be at the airport at least three hours before international departures." She turned her gaze to the Rollaboard waiting by the door and she would not look up at him, not even when he hugged her goodbye.

9

Quiet filled the house. Vera tiptoed across the Maginot Line. Dylan and Anne Mom were hugging each other on his bed beneath his fire-truck comforter. It was hard to figure out who was comforting whom, but they would need all the comfort they could get out of each other. They wouldn't need her, Vera thought. They would be "devastated" for a while, but then they would continue as Mommy and son. As she hovered at the doorjamb, they did not even notice her.

Vera went back to her room and put on her "spy" hoodie. She took the ancient elevator to the basement and snuck out of their apartment building. She hunched her shoulders in. The weather was "crisp" and she refused to sweat despite the swift progress of her legs. The streets passed by her, one by one by one. Then the avenues. Then the streets again. A MOTH was starting on another avenue today and she marched alongside it past the people screaming at the silent people, past the silent people smiling at the screamers, past the anger and the laughter, past the policemen looking bored, past the immigrants selling corn with a kind of spicy mayonnaise (her father's favorite, even though it gave him diarrhea).

"Remember, Yoon-a. Now that you're a spy, you're the one who's different. Not the people around you."

She had to be Yoon-a Choi. She had to be. She was definitely the one who was different. She had been different at school, but now with Yumi as her "best friend forever" she was no longer alone, at least until Yumi's parents' tour of duty in America was over (so maybe it wasn't "forever"). But now she was different in every other way that mattered. Because she had no family.

I am Yoon-a Choi, she thought.

And then she thought about it some more.

Choi was a Korean last name.

,

The doorman at Yumi's building was not "perplexed" by her solitary appearance and sent her right up. Maybe he had "seen it all" already, like many people in the city had. Yumi's parents were busy being diplomats that weekend, attending important functions, so a babysitter opened the door, an elderly Asian woman. "Oh," she said, gravely.

A very concerned Yumi led Vera into her room, past the NO SISTERS ALLOWED sign. Her "difficult" sister was having a playdate in the other room and there was a lot of Dylan-esque squealing coming out of there. "Oh my God," Yumi said, sounding very adult re: Vera's sudden appearance. "What happened?"

"Iris Choi," Vera said. "Can you look that up?"

Yumi got out her device. The room was slightly spinning around Vera, but she noticed that all of the debate corkboards had been taken down. That part of my childhood is over, she thought.

They plugged in "Iris Choi" and the College of Fading

Repute. There were far fewer results than off the other searches. There was still a lot of stuff about the eye doctor who had worked with irises and attended the College of Fading Repute, but then they found a photograph.

It was definitely from the college, because it featured the kind of "edifice" that colleges had, built out of stones that had aged well, but in this case you could definitely feel the repute fading. It was the ledge of an "academic" building most likely and three students were sitting on it. Three students with their legs dangling off the ledge, smiling with their teeth and their eyes like Aunt Cecile did before she caught her awful flu.

"Boris Argunoff, Iris Choi, and Jeff Levine-Straussberg," the caption read.

Vera looked at the happy young woman in the middle and sighed. She was wearing the kind of striped "French" shirt thing that they had not seen worn in Paris at all and billowing jeans. She had such a large forehead—come to think of it, she had such a very large head, very much like Vera's. She scanned down. "Iris Choi is a double major in psychology and a self-designed concentration in futurism and originally hails from Youngstown, Ohio."

The elderly Asian woman knocked on their door. "Lunch," she said.

They were eating a Japanese fall classic, Yumi explained, *kuri gohan,* or chestnut rice. It was delicious, but of course neither girl could concentrate on her meal. Yumi's sister and her playdate were pretending to be penguins for some reason and everything they said was in their own "penguin language," which quickly got annoying.

"So how are you?" Vera asked her friend. She remembered not to make it all about herself even if something as momentous as finding your mom mom was happening right this very moment.

"I'm fine," Yumi said. "Just fine." They really enjoyed talking like adults, especially in front of the little girls pretending to be penguins. Now that Yumi and Stephen were an "item," the first item in the history of their fifth grade, Vera felt adult just being next to someone like Yumi.

"How's it going with Stephen?" Vera asked.

Yumi rolled her eyes. "He's a handful," she said.

They "scarfed down" their chestnut rice and asked the old lady if they could be excused. Back in the bedroom, they set about finding out everything they could about Iris Choi. They typed "feverishly," passing the device from one to the other. Iris Choi must have been a spy herself, because she had stayed hidden from the Internet, beyond the photo of her with her two friends, their legs dangling carefree at the College of Fading Repute. But Vera was going to find her. Her mom mom was going to make her a Korean fall classic and it would taste even better than the chestnut rice the old lady had reheated in the kitchen.

Although there were no mentions of Iris Choi, a number of Chois did live in the Youngstown area. Some attended or taught at the local public college. "Maybe your mom's parents still live there?" Yumi said.

"How old would they have to be?" Vera wondered. The girls looked up when women had children.

"I think they had them earlier back then," Yumi said, and Vera did a lot of calculations on a whiteboard.

They worked for another hour. There were three groups of elderly Chois in the area, two couples and a solitary one. "What do we do?" Vera asked.

"We have to call them," Yumi said.

Vera's vertigo returned. "I can't," she said.

"I'll do it," Yumi said. Vera touched the galaxy leggings of her brave best friend forever.

They dialed the first number. It rang and rang, until a woman picked up, breathing heavily into the phone. Thank God, old people still picked up phones. "Hi," Yumi said. "So sorry for the disturbance. Are you the mother of Iris Choi?"

"What?" the old woman said. "Who is this? What Iris?"

"So sorry!" Yumi blurted out and pressed the button to end the call.

The girls looked at each other. "Are we breaking a law?" Vera asked. She wanted to follow all the laws, unlike her father. She pictured him boarding the airplane to Budapest right about now. Would Other Vera pay for Business Class, or would her father finally discover Family Class all on his own? She told herself to stop thinking of him.

Yumi dialed the second number. A woman picked up right away, her accent heavier than the first woman's. "Yes," she said. "Hello."

"Hi," Yumi said. "So sorry for the disturbance. Are you the mother of Iris Choi?"

The line went dead, or at least seemed to. The duration of the call registered on the black screen and Vera counted the numbers as if they were the streets leading up to school. "Who is this?" the woman said. When frozen Yumi and Vera failed to answer, she finally said, "Yes, I am the mother."

Vera hit the disconnect button and put her hand to her mouth. "Are you okay?" Yumi asked.

Vera scanned her friend's face, the hair pooling at her shoulders. She wanted to be like her, but she also wanted to be herself. Anne Mom said she would find herself at Swarthmore, but maybe she could "short-circuit" the process.

She looked at Yumi's device. Hun and Carol Choi were the names of her grandparents. The screen of the device turned black and rang. Carol Choi was calling them back! "Don't pick up!" Vera screamed. "Don't pick up!"

"Are you sure?" Yumi asked.

"I'm not ready," Vera said.

Yumi turned off the device completely. "Now they'll be worried," she said.

"I have to go see them," Vera said.

"In Ohio?" Yumi asked. "But how? Will they let you get on a plane by yourself?" Perhaps this was possible in Japan, which was a very safe society. "Could you ask your other mom?"

But Vera couldn't do that. Not right now. "I don't know what to do," she confessed. She hadn't meant to sound as sad as Anne Mom.

"We'll find a way," Yumi said. "We won the debate and we found your grandparents. We can figure out anything."

,

When she got home before dinnertime, Anne Mom and Dylan were still in his bedroom. She had not been missed at all.

19.

She Had to "Hatch a Plan"

She couldn't sleep. How could she when all of life passed like a dream? Now that their father was gone, Dylan even refused to drop his pants. So he had always dropped them not to gross out Vera and other people but to be raffish for his father. How much of his behavior could be explained by their famous father? How much of hers? Anne Mom had said that Vera worshipped him. But she was an atheist, through and through.

They ate dinner silently, sullenly, Anne Mom "peppering" them with questions about their day. Dylan said he had gotten into a "real fight" with Stephen because Stephen didn't want to throw the mud bowl at him anymore or get into a slapping contest.

"That's because he has a girlfriend," Vera said.

"*You* have a girlfriend," Dylan "shot back."

"Could you please tell Dylan to stop being stupid," Vera said.

"All of us have to adjust to life being different from now on," Anne Mom said in her Boston Brahmin voice. "And that's going to make us uncomfortable at times. I can't fault either of you. I can just ask you, politely, to stop."

Vera looked at the couch upon which her father used to lie with his phone, sometimes even during dinner. She looked down at the tiny hairs starting to rise up and down her elbows. How would she ever get rid of Daddy's inheritance?

9

Who would protect her from the things she needed protecting from? Her insomnia fueled her anxiety and her anxiety fueled her insomnia "and on and on and on ad infinitum." She wiped some of the grime off the fire extinguisher with a wet piece of toilet paper at school and Ron the Guard yelled at her. She saw a bus coming her way as she was about to be picked up by Stella, and she stuck her foot out onto the street, just for a second, just to test what it would be like to have something so huge and monstrous bear down on her. She snuck out to the Maginot Line every night to touch all the burners in the kitchen, make sure they were off, but also hoping, for no reason she could explain, that one of them would be on, and that the pain would jolt her awake, even though insomnia was what made her life miserable.

A terrible thing happened at school; beyond terrible,

outlandish even. She got a C on a vocab quiz in English language arts. The quiz consisted of simple words, or at least they were simple for her school. "Succession." "Elimination." "Inland." Words she should have known in her sleep, had she gotten any. News of Vera's C traveled around the school quickly, that's how unexpected it was. At recess, Vera sat with her Yoon-a Choi spy book, the one she had reread a dozen times in the last week, while the Populars goofed around on their bench and Stephen and Yumi took a walk around the perimeter of the playground, talking seriously about love.

All of a sudden, Principal Bellavista's big butt had "scooched" next to her small one. He had a big clipboard that he liked to carry and a whistle around his neck. "Is everything okay, Vera?" he asked.

"Yes," she said.

"I was a little surprised by your vocab grade."

"I'm sorry," Vera said.

"Don't be sorry," the principal said. "Just trying to figure out what happened. You probably have a bigger vocab hoard than me. Though I was always a math guy."

"In what's left of Britain, they say 'maths,'" Vera said. "Probably in the other parts, too," she allowed.

"I suppose you're right," the principal said. "My job is to look out for red flags. Is everything okay at home?"

"My father went away for a while," Vera said. "He went to Budapest. The cost of living is lower there."

"I see," Principal Bellavista said.

"It's also the capital of the Commonwealth of Illiberal States," Vera said. "But maybe it's a coincidence." She had read just about anything one could about Budapest, even though she had to get her father out of her mind.

"I know your mom is going to want to discuss your C with me," Principal Bellavista said. "Get it up to a B minus at least."

"I know," Vera said. "But maybe we can wait before telling her? I was having a bad day. I bet if I retake the test, I'll get an A. This isn't a 'cry for help.'"

Principal Bellavista smiled. "Can you just promise me you'll talk to Mrs. S. this week? Her door is always—"

"I know," Vera said. "I know."

❧

Getting a C in vocab was a huge mistake, she now realized. She needed Anne Mom to lower her guard and think she was doing just fine, maybe even concentrate entirely on Dylan. She and Yumi and apparently now even Stephen were "hatching a plan." It turned out that Stephen had many devices and despite his everyday "sloth" had a keen appreciation of how artificial intelligences worked.

She needed to get to Ohio as quickly as possible, before Mom Mom died. Vera wondered if she was in the famous Cleveland Clinic, very close to Youngstown. Maybe that's why the Chois had decided to live there, because she had some exotic disease that could easily lead to cancer and necessitated "proximity" to one of America's best hospitals. That's why she went to college so nearby as well, just in case her illness "flared." Iris Choi had always been very fragile, very special, but then she met her father, and her father just didn't know what to do with that specialness, and that's why Vera was stuck without a family.

At recess, Yumi passed her a note, and even though she wasn't wearing her spy hoodie, Vera slipped it into her red-checkered skirt and ran off to the bathroom with it. Yumi's handwriting was exceptional, it was one subject in which she would definitely kick Vera's butt, but it wasn't a subject that was graded, thankfully. Vera read the lovely cursive while a third grader peed "insolently" in the next stall.

Stephen is researching the kind of AI Stella is.

He thinks he understands her "language model."

Stephen does not think Stella is very sophissticated [sic].
From what you say she just repeats what other people say and tries to do the same emotions.

Stephen does not think Stella can tell your mother's "image" from her actual face.

Stephen wants to know if there are any portable AIs in your house that can imitate you're [sic, poor Yumi] mother Anne's voice.

End transmission.

Yes, I get it, Yumi, Vera thought as she read the note over and over. Underneath it all, Stephen was very smart. Good for you, Yumi, for finding a boyfriend so smart, handsome, and rich. As thankful as she was for all of their help, she shared Dylan's worry that her favorite person at school had found a more inspiring friend slash partner than herself. But she couldn't "concern" herself with that now. She had to get to Ohio.

§

"Respected Kaspie," she said, trying to sound Korean and probably overdoing it.

"Good evening, Su-won," Kaspie said. "Shall we play a game?" He started moving the pieces to make her "white." Someone had to, now that her father was gone.

"I wanted to ask you something."

"Of course, Su-won."

"Is there anything more important than finding my mother? She's *hanbok-sarah* and everything."

"Hanguk-*saram*. No, it is very important."

"I think I've found her," Vera said. "And I have to visit her because she's very sick. But I can't let Anne Bradford know. Because she might not let me go."

"I see," Kaspie said.

"Respected Kaspie, I need you to imitate Anne Bradford's voice to convince Stella the Car to drive me to Ohio. Please do so for my family." Vera bowed to the chessboard.

"I am not sure this is safe," Kaspie said after some thinking. "I think you should consult with your provisional mother."

"So you won't help me?" Vera asked. "Yumi's boyfriend, Stephen, said you can probably mimic any human voice. You have the language modules."

"I cannot allow harm to come to the people who use me."

"What harm?" Vera said. "I'm going to see my real family. When you told me my father was a traitor, you destroyed any family I have here. He fled to Budapest because Anne Mom could have turned him in. You're responsible, Kaspie! And now you want to keep me away from Hanguk-*saram*? What would Dr. Oh of the Korea Advanced Institute of Science and Technology say? Maybe you should call *your* father!"

She said this, but she also said more. Her debating skills were excellent, but also she had learned the art of manipulation from Anne Mom and her father and at least three of her five living grandparents. To his disadvantage, Kaspie had not learned this art. He countered some of her arguments but then conceded that she might find more safety "among your own people." He proved, in the end, to be a good "nationalist," the kind her father had always derided.

❡

Vera's scarlet letter, her C in English language arts, would be posted online the next day, and after Anne Mom saw it she would be worried about Vera and watch her "like a hawk." Or, and this worried Vera all the more, she might have already given up on Vera entirely to focus on her biological son. She did not wish to find out which option was true. They had to act right away.

A lot of this depended on Yumi being able to sneak out of her house in the middle of the night and make it the twenty-five blocks to the garage below Vera's building where Stella spent the night. Sneaking out of her building was not difficult for Yumi, as there were many "egresses." It was a fancy building and even had a sad, barely working waterfall on one level. As for walking through the center of the city all alone at midnight, Yumi was blessed with her tremendous height. Her father, it was said, had played basketball semiprofessionally back in Japan while being a scholar. It really was an incredible family, especially now that Vera was losing her father's distaste for athletes.

Vera had spent her last dinner in the city looking at Dylan and wanting to hold his hand and tell him it was "going to be all right." She nudged him with her elbow, hoping he would punch it. But he just stared at the row of "pigs in a blanket" he had assembled on the plate in front of him, perhaps to form the letters *SOS* in some kind of alien-from-outer-space language (although he wasn't all that great at English, Vera thought), and said, "Leave me alone." She pictured having sangria and razor clams at a restaurant with him one day when they were much older. Maybe if Five-Three passed he would be given some kind of sash to wear. "Can you believe everything we went through?" she would say re: the crazy year their father left and she ran away. But that would be in the future, what about now? Who would do his geography homework to-morrow? Who would help him find Budapest on a map? She did not want to be a terrible older sister, but she needed to see Mom Mom before she died. One day he would understand why she did what she did and they wouldn't have to fight over the check the way her father and the Seal always had because they were "immigrants with finite resources."

She said goodbye to the Maginot Line with its copies of *The Power Broker, Their Eyes Were Watching God,* and *Kindertransport,* blew an "Aunt Cecile–style kiss" to Dylan in his room, and snuck out with her spare key, taking the elevator to the garage. At exactly midnight she opened the side door to the garage from within to see Yumi's smiling face. Thank God she was safe. They had checked the crime rates on every block between their apartment buildings to ensure the least criminalized passage. "Are you ready?" Yumi said.

"We should say goodbye now, before you become Anne Bradford," Vera said.

"Goodbye," Yumi said. They hugged. Is there really any

difference between having a sister and a best friend for-ever? Vera wondered. Kaspie said that "blood" was impor-tant and maybe that's why she was looking for Mom Mom, but then again she had a sister in Yumi, and their blood came from opposite sides of the Korea Strait.

"Do you think you'll marry Stephen?" Vera asked.

"Probably," Yumi said. "But I want to have a powerful career, too. And he'll have to move to Japan. I wouldn't want to live here forever."

Vera was happy Yumi didn't want to become a Tradwife like Anne Mom.

"But you'll come back, right?" Yumi asked.

"It depends on how my mommy is doing. How sick she is."

Yumi nodded. It was time for them to become opera-tional and execute their "ruse." Yumi put on the mask she had printed out, which featured Anne Mom's face in full living color. According to suddenly smart Stephen, Stella the Car recognized basic facial structure but was too lazy to scan pupils or irises. (Like Iris Choi! Vera thought hap-pily of the pun.) She took Kaspie out of the bag where she had stowed her passport and toothbrush as they ap-proached sleeping Stella.

Vera touched the front door handle. "Wake up, Stella," she said.

Stella's lights flicked on. "Oh my God, do you know what time it is?" Stella said in full Anne Mom mode.

"Stella," Kaspie spoke in Anne Mom's voice. He mirrored Anne Mom perfectly. "We have an emergency."

"Great," Stella said. "Fun never ends around here."

"The pipes burst in our apartment and everything is flooded."

Stella sighed. "I have a list of nearby hotels—"

"I need you to drive Vera to her aunt's house in Youngstown, Ohio." Kaspie read out the address in Anne Mom's deep voice.

This was a "make or break" moment for their ruse. If Stella was smart, she would ask why only Vera was to be driven to Ohio and not, for example, her brother. She would ask why she had never heard of an aunt in the Midwest.

But Stella was not smart. Even though she had cost a lot more than Kaspie, she was not a graduate of the Korea Advanced Institute of Science and Technology and had in fact been made in America. "Ohio?" she said. "All the way in Ohio? That's three hundred ninety-five miles away. Just wonderful. Calculating route."

"We'll see you in a few days once the pipes are fixed," Yumi slash Kaspie slash Anne Mom said and Vera hugged her friend who was really her sister who was pretending to be her provisional mother. "One more thing, Stella," Yumi said. "Could you please turn off tracking? I read an article about how children in autonomous vehicles can be traced and human trafficked."

"Fine." Stella sighed.

"I love you," Yumi whispered into Vera's ear.

❧

Stella opened the garage door and within minutes they were on the empty highway. She saw Yumi's darkened building, hoping she wouldn't get caught and get in terrible trouble with her parents (or have to reveal their plot and call Anne Mom), and then she saw the island in the middle of the river, lying there like a lightless cruise ship that had run aground centuries ago.

"Octagon," she said.

20.

She Had to Make It to Ohio

"What a delectable morning," Stella said. "Kind of reminds me of the sunrise over the Seongsan Ilchulbong."

Vera stirred herself awake. The darkness was receding. By the dawn's early light. That our flag was still there.

"So," Stella said. "How's the chess going? Any good moves I should know about?" Vera yawned. Stella was always going to be Stella. She would imitate a fly if it landed on her.

Vera wanted to capture the mix of sadness, happiness, and uncertainty inside her. "Could you play my father's favorite music?" Vera asked the car.

"Playing Bach, *The Goldberg Variations*, BWV 988, 1981 recording," Stella said. The music filled the cabin. Her speakers were beautiful.

"How far away are we?" Vera asked.

"Cycle Through checkpoint at the Ohio border in

forty-five minutes. After that I estimate about forty-one more minutes to arrival."

Vera looked at America passing before her. She had already seen the great cities of the world, but she had never seen the interior of her own country. She had been to Maine, but that wasn't the same. Grams lived very well there, but she also had "one foot" in Boston in a grand apartment beneath that city's skyscraper.

The country scrolled past her as the Bach filled her with "melancholy." She remembered, for no particular reason, that her father sometimes used what he said was a funny phrase from his youth, "babies having babies." Was he talking about himself and her real mom? Some people never stopped being babies. She could hear the pianist Glenn Gould humming like a baby past the melody he was playing vigorously on the piano. He was so in love with the music he was making, he couldn't help himself. Everyone should love their work like that. Would she love her STEM as much when the time came to be a woman in it?

Her monkey brain was going, but she didn't want to let it stop. Let it carry her wherever it wanted to go. She saw Yumi making the monkey sound when she had said that Lincoln had been the Ape of Illinois, which was just two states past Ohio. Their first joke together.

By the side of the highway, she saw an American flag so big it managed to blot out the horizon. As they got closer she realized it was for a dealership selling Korean cars.

Anne Mom would say that was a good omen. But according to Kaspie, they weren't related by blood, so it almost didn't count. Her father was related to her by blood, but he was in Budapest being "illiberal" as he probably listened to the same Bach she was listening to now. Who else did she have by blood? There was Grandpa Boris and Baba Tanya, but they couldn't protect her. They couldn't even leave their house except to steal leaf blowers under cover of night. Would her mom mom protect her before she died? Would she tell her to go somewhere safe where people loved her? Back to Korea? Would her grandparents protect her? Her grandpa was named Hun, as in "Attila the." She saw him riding down the hill on a horse covered with a bejeweled blanket ready to throw a spear at some European. Her father had always blamed the Mongols for how Russia had turned out while acknowledging the "inherent racism" of such a statement. She would have to acknowledge it, too. She would have to grow up so fast to reach the "age of majority," still eight years away. And after that she would be able to protect herself.

,

"We are approaching the Cycle Through station at the Ohio border," Stella said. "Do you have your passport or birth certificate ready?"

They were stuck in a line outside the border station, beneath a giant billboard that showed two happy women "cycling through" on a tandem bicycle. Vera pictured it as her and Yumi. There was a male-only lane that zipped past them, but cars with women and girls had to wait for inspection.

When their turn came, a man with a mustache like nobody in the city had motioned to Stella to roll down her windows and open her trunk. He wore a big gray hat and a black tie and looked very professional. He shone a flashlight into Stella, even though the sun had already been up for an hour. "Hi, honey," he said. "Where you going?"

Vera gave him her passport. "I'm going to see my aunt in the great state of Ohio," she said, not wanting to "trip up" the story she had presented to Stella. "She lives in Youngstown."

"That sounds nice," the policeman said. "You're not being trafficked in this car or anything? Could you turn the music down please?" Stella lowered *The Goldberg Variations*.

"No," Vera said, unsure of what that meant. "This is our family car, Stella."

"No one's been grooming you?"

"My aunt Cecile took me to a hair-grooming place. We had a smoothie."

"No one's been grooming you to be gay or trans?"

"I don't think so. But I'm not supposed to think in binaries."

The policeman was shuffling through the many entry

stamps in her passport. "Korea," he said. "Is that North or South?"

"South!" Vera said, proudly.

"Says here you're ten."

"I'll be eleven in eight months."

"You look a little small to be ten. Are you menstruating already, honey?"

Menstruating? What did that mean? Vera's vocabulary failed her, just like it had during the English language arts test where she had been given her C.

"Yes?" she said.

"Do you know what that means?" He pointed his useless flashlight in the direction of her "private area." "Are you bleeding down there?"

"Down where?"

"Between your legs."

"I got scraped there once," she said, meaning between her thighs after she had fallen off a bike that her father had tried to teach her to ride.

"So the way this works, you can either pee in a cup or we can do a Holmes."

"I really need to pee," Vera said.

"I'll be honest with you," the nice policeman said, "it's not super sanitary around here. The Holmes will take just a second. It's like a tiny pinprick on your finger, nothing like a shot at the doctor's."

"Okay," Vera said.

"And you can pee when you get to your aunt's house. Youngstown is super close."

"Okay," Vera said again. She was following all the rules like she always had except for the ruse she and Yumi had pulled.

The finger prick hurt like a really bad mosquito bite up in the countryside. The policeman put the needle into a little machine. "Darn it," he said. "Sometimes these don't work so good. Still better than peeing in a cup though. Can we try it one more time?"

"Different finger?" Vera asked. She was feeling dizzy again for some reason.

"Yeah," the policeman said. "Different finger."

"I hope it's not my fault," Vera said.

"Nah, it's these things." He pricked her middle finger, she was used to pain by now, and "ran" the thing again in his machine. A long piece of paper flapped out. "Okay," he said. "This is your receipt. So when you leave Ohio at the border when you're headed back east, you have to present it one more time at a Cycle Through station, and they'll give you another Holmes and you'll be good to go."

"Thank you very much," Vera said.

"You're very welcome. Here, let me get you into the express lane out so that you can get to your aunt faster." He waved them past some other cars and back onto the highway. Although two of her fingers stung, Vera thought he had been a very nice policeman. Stella turned the music up again and Vera tried to read the "receipt" for her blood even though she couldn't understand most of it. One thing was for certain, they were in Ohio now.

Her grandparents lived on something called New Road, which Vera thought was a very modern and optimistic name. They passed an establishment named Trax Restaurant and Lounge. Trax like "train tracks," Vera thought. "The wrong side of the tracks." Stop thinking! They pulled up to the curb of a strange kind of house. It had what looked like long brown panels on the second floor but lots of brick on the first, though not the kind of ancient brick the College of Fading Repute was built of. And the house was connected to other houses of a similar type. Was this a town house, then? Even Grams didn't live in a town house when she was in Boston.

"This house is barely worth ninety thousand dollars," Stella sneered in her most obnoxious city mode, dashing Vera's dreams of generational wealth.

"Stay here," Vera said to her car.

"I wish the president could do something more about human trafficking," Stella said, thoughtfully. "I've just been reading a lot of posts about how Hollywood stars are grooming and trafficking children. I hope no Hollywood star is grooming and trafficking you." Stella had bad informational hygiene, Vera thought. Was she imitating the policeman at the Cycle Through now?

Vera walked up a path leading past scraggly grass and

the leaves that had started falling in the great state of Ohio. Next door, someone had already set up a pumpkin, but the Chois liked to keep things minimal.

She rang the doorbell with one of her scarred fingertips. No one answered for a while. She rang again and again. She rang until her own ears rang. The interior door opened and then the sad-looking white outer door. A woman in large glasses rimmed with gold looked down at her. She brought the glasses closer to her nose and then staggered back. She staggered forward, holding on to the doorframe. "Uh-muh-na," she said, covering her mouth with her hand. "Uhmuhna, uhmuhna, uhmuhna."

Vera didn't understand her, but she did.

21.

She Had to Find Out the Truth About Mom Mom

The Choi house was very much like Grandpa Boris and Baba Tanya's house, except instead of menorahs they had oily paintings of many Jesuses with many lambs. Outdoor footwear was also prohibited here, and there was a kind of ordered messiness, many papers and "sundry" objects packed into transparent boxes, old electronics heaped on top of one another, plastic covers on the "ornate" yet inexpensive couches. Maybe all immigrants lived in essentially the same house, Vera thought. The main difference was that the Chois were vaccinated and they could eat together inside the house. Vera's sole experiences of the Shmulkin "manse" (as her father derisively called it) were conducted on trips from the back porch to the bathroom while wearing disposable slippers Baba Tanya stored up for the occasion.

They sat at a table in the kitchen, which looked out on a tiny backyard, most of it taken up by a gigantic unit which apparently air-conditioned the house. Vera was eating a short-rib stew very "voraciously." The meat was the kind adults said "melted off the bone" and it came with radishes, carrots, and even chestnuts just like Yumi's chestnut rice! It also contained many little pimples of fat, the opposite of what Anne Mom encouraged her to eat.

Vera's grandparents were watching Vera eat very intently, and very silently. Carol did not have tears in her eyes, but they were somewhere inside her because every time she breathed there was a rush of liquid and air in her nose and in her throat. Hun sat there as if he had been a soldier and had just returned from a long battle and was contemplating all the comrades he had lost while celebrating his own return home. This was the story Vera managed to invent as she packed her mouth full of meat and chestnuts and carrots and radishes, ignoring the glass of cold Ohio water that sat next to her plate. As she was eating, she was as "cognizant" of the rise and fall of her breath as she would have been during one of Anne Mom's meditations. She could almost see what the British voice in her earbuds would describe as the "liquid sunlight" melting within her, the general state of being present and okay that had so long eluded her and Anne Mom, though God knows she tried.

I'm safe now, she thought. And soon my real mother will come.

Eventually Vera stopped eating and burped very loudly, the kind of burp Dylan would have surely appreciated. Both her grandparents laughed and Carol even clapped. "This means you like it," she said.

"I love it," Vera said.

"It is called *galbi-jjim*," Carol said. "Very nice for the weather right now."

"It's enchanting," Vera said. The grandparents perhaps did not understand this word, but it did not matter.

"You know," Carol said, "it was the favorite dish of your mommy."

They sat there in silence. The *M* word—"mommy"—had just been spoken aloud, and Vera wondered if she could delay learning what she had to learn, so she could be just a granddaughter and not a daughter for a little while longer. But she couldn't.

"Speaking of my mommy," she said, trying to be as adult as possible, because adults seemed to love her for it, or at least some of them did.

"Would you like to see some photos?" Hun asked.

"Yes," she said. Although she wanted more than photos.

Hun and Carol walked her over to a credenza in the hallway. "Here it is, your family," Carol said.

There were so many photos that Vera felt the familiar burst of vertigo when she was overstimulated. She flapped her hands, but just once, so that it would look like she was shaking something off of them, water maybe. She didn't want her grandparents to get the wrong impression about her.

"So here is June Emo getting master's degree at Purdue," Hun said.

"What's *emo*?" Vera asked. There were some "emo" kids in the middle school adjoining her own, but they mostly wore weird makeup.

"It means 'aunt' in Korean," Carol said. "Your father didn't send you for Korea classes?"

"No," Vera said.

"Your daddy promised us," Hun said.

"My father's very complicated," Vera explained. She turned back toward the photos, because she didn't want to talk about him.

"Yes," Hun said, "Purdue is a good regional college. Strong in STEM and engineering." Vera liked that her grandparents spoke the same language of statuses as her other family, even though they lived in a house that cost under a hundred thousand dollars.

"June Emo is a car designer in Michigan," Carol said. Vera could tell by her body language that she was proud.

"Maybe she designed my car, Stella," Vera said. "Speaking of June, I had an enemy named Joon-hee at school. But then I became friends with Yumi and now she is not an enemy anymore, though not really a friend. Joon-hee is very angry that my friend Yumi is dating Stephen. What goes around comes around, they say."

Her grandparents smiled at all the words coming out of her.

"These are your cousins," Hun said.

Vera skipped past the boys—she already had a brother—and looked at the girl, who was maybe seven or eight, the youngest. She was sitting atop a man who must have been her father, a "burly" man in a baseball cap and with a "ginger" beard reaching down to his chest. Behind her was some kind of nature, a waterfall only slightly better than the one Yumi had in her building. Ohio was not a delectable state. June Emo was looking up at her daughter with "loving eyes," and the daughter looked like she was about to explode from happiness. Vera felt the jealousy in all of her body. Her own father had never "hoisted" her up on his shoulders. He had said he was too old to lift her. And Anne Mom did not have those eyes for her, only for Dylan.

She tried to think of every way she was better than her cousin. The smarts she had, the statuses. But none of it helped. She wished she had had her life.

No, she told herself. Wrong! Wrong! Love her. You must love her. You must love your new cousin.

In the corner of the shelf, "out of sight, out of mind," there was another photograph, once again of a woman graduating from college, and Vera automatically recognized the crest of the College of Fading Repute, and then she recognized half of herself. Her mother stood all alone, without the family that Vera thought would always surround you in graduation photos, and she stared into the camera with both a crinkled smile around her eyes and the trace of a sneer along her full lips. Vera's father frequently had that look in photographs. Did he teach her mother how to do that in college?

"She's beautiful," Vera said. But she didn't really mean it. Because how could a "trite" word like "beautiful" describe anything when it came to her mother. Her mother could have had two heads and it wouldn't have mattered. Vera would have uttered the same trite words, and then the same feeling of loneliness would have surged in her diaphragm and breast, the real stuff that lived inside her instead of the Englishman's liquid sunlight.

"Yes," Carol said, re: Vera's mother's, her daughter's, beauty.

"I wish I could come up with some other words to say about her," Vera said. "I keep a diary of all the words I still need to learn and understand, but I left it back home."

"Your mother also kept a diary of words," Carol said. "So similar."

"Really?" Vera said. "She also liked words?"

"When we first came to America, we didn't know the language," Hun said.

"My mommy didn't know English?"

"No."

"She was like my father that way, I guess," Vera said, allowing her to feel something for the man named Igor Shmulkin.

"I can bring you her book of words," Hun said.

Book of Words, Vera liked how that sounded. Her grandfather went to the living room, where she heard him slamming through one set of wooden drawers and then another one. She found herself looking at her hands, still stained with the last school day's ink (she needed a shower), as if they contained an answer. Finally, he returned with a withered notebook that was coming apart in several ways. The book had a Korean Air logo on it. Vera opened it, holding it with both hands so that it wouldn't disintegrate. The handwriting was delectable, in both English and in her mom mom's mother tongue.

Mom Mom had written words in English in one column and the Korean translations in another. Which meant she had known Korean well, had had a life in it, a life that was interrupted. "That is moving," Vera whispered to herself, both understanding and not understanding the meaning of what she felt. "I am moved," she tried again to herself.

The words were so much simpler than the words in the

Things I Still Need to Know Diary. Her mother had started with so much less than her.

> *Money.*
> *Spend.*
> *Spending.*
> *Discount.*
> *Bus.*
> *Ticket.*
> *Transfer.*
> *Money transfer.*
> *Emergency.*
> *Kidney.*
> *Liver.*
> *Diabetes.*
> *Library.*
> *Due date.*
> *Fine (penalty).*
> *Foreign language section.*

"How old was she when she wrote this?" Vera asked Carol.

"Maybe eight?" her grandmother said.

"No, no, seven," Hun said. "We still live in Irvine then."

Vera put her fingers to the words. She traced them. She wished she had better penmanship instead of her Dylan-grade handwriting. She wished she could show her mother all the new words she had learned. If Mom Mom had majored in something as difficult as psychology and "futurism" at the College of Fading Repute, she probably already knew most of them.

"Where are the other pictures of my mother?" Vera asked.

"There are baby and school photos in the basement," Hun said. "If you like I can get."

"I mean more recent photos," Vera said.

The grandparents looked at each other and Carol said something in Korean and then Hun said something in Korean and Vera realized she had been studying the wrong language at the Language Larder, but it was too late and now she would never know whatever her grandparents didn't want her to know.

"What do you mean by more recent photo?" Hun finally asked. "We don't understand." He put his arm around his wife's non-waist, which could have given Anne Mom's a "run for its money." He's protecting her, Vera thought. But are they also protecting me? And from what?

"I know my mommy's been very sick," Vera said. "And it's not nice to take pictures of people when they're sick."

"Who said she is sick?" Carol wanted to know.

"My father."

The grandparents said nothing. Maybe her father did

not have many fans in Ohio either. "Please sit down and I will get you a glass of water," Carol said. "Or do you like milk?"

"Oat milk?"

"Not oat," Hun said. "From a cow."

"Water is fine."

22.

She Had to Find Out the Truth About Her Mother and Her Father

She sat down with her grandparents at the table. The smell of the *galbi-jjim* was very strong despite the bowl being in the sink. The large air-conditioning unit taking up half the backyard made a lot of noise, and it was the only noise Vera heard for a while.

Hun spoke. He had a very small mouth with very fine lips, nothing like the Attila the Hun Vera had imagined. He was short, almost as short as his wife. Her grandmother had a big head like Vera's, and her hair was cut in a similar way, which made her look much younger than she probably was. Vera was thinking all of these things because she didn't want to hear what Hun was saying. But she heard him nonetheless.

"Your mother has gone to heaven," he said.

Once again Vera thought of the empty place in the sky

Father Chase had tried to convince her existed at the Sunday school in Maine. Of course, without gravity, everyone in heaven would fall straight to hell, a word Anne Mom did not like. But that's how the universe worked, Vera thought. You wanted to believe someone was in a pretty place like heaven, but really everybody, herself included, was living in hell.

"I'm sorry I didn't make it in time to say goodbye," Vera said, keeping her own tears in her throat because she had to be an adult for her grandparents.

"What do you mean?" Carol said.

"Was she at the Cleveland Clinic?" Vera asked.

"She was," Hun began and then stopped. "She was at a different kind of facility. She was very unhappy."

"What kind of facility?" Vera asked.

"It's not important," Carol said. "I'm sorry your mommy didn't get to see what a big smart girl you are."

"Was she unhappy because of me? I know I wasn't 'planned.'"

"No!" both grandparents shouted.

"Because of my father?"

"No," Carol finally said, but softly.

"I should have come earlier," Vera said, looking at her empty plate.

"But, Vera," Carol said. "Your mommy passed away right after you were born. Maybe just six months after."

This news landed in Vera's chest and stayed there. Her

grandmother reached over to touch her hand. "I'm sorry," her grandmother said. "I am usually not very emotional."

"So she didn't have cancer?" Vera whispered. "She was just unhappy?"

Her grandparents did not answer her questions.

"If she didn't have cancer," Vera reasoned, "then who does? My father said someone had cancer."

And then she remembered herself getting an acting lesson in the wooden auditorium on the railroad trestle hanging over the city streets with the cars all going uptown, the red lights on their butts all lit up.

"You're not that old!" Vera had said, trying to break up Aunt Cecile's fugue.

"I'm not," Aunt Cecile had said. "That's what's so sad about it, I guess. Or so they say."

"Oh," Vera said now to her grandparents, but really to herself.

How much more could her heart break? A lot. It could and would break a lot more. There were, contrary to science, an infinite number of atriums and ventricles.

Her grandparents spoke some more in Korean and then Carol said, "There is a letter we can show you."

"From my mother?"

"No," Hun said. "Your father."

He left to fetch it, and soon after, Carol got up and walked out of the kitchen, too. She can't handle being alone with me, Vera thought. I shouldn't have pushed about my dead mother. I should have just stayed silent and admired the pictures of my cousins and my aunt. My *emo*. What have I done? She heard more wooden drawers being slammed. How many drawers would have to suffer until she learned all of the truth?

Her grandparents walked back together, Carol blowing her nose, making sounds like the recorder Vera had been forced to play in fourth grade, the one that still awaited Dylan. Hun placed a letter encased in clear plastic on the kitchen table before her. This was the way Anne Mom kept all of her documents, too, the deed to the country house, for example.

"If you don't want to read, you don't have to," Carol said.

"But maybe you should anyway," Hun said.

Carol spoke more terse words in Korean. Vera did not want them to fight and started reading immediately. The letter was printed on a thin, almost transparent piece of paper, like the kind that came out of the printer in the formerly parental bedroom, not the Icelandic paper stock her father had dreamed of for his failed magazine.

Dear Carol and Hun,

Greetings!
All is well here, the weather is improving, and I have gotten a promotion to senior assistant editor at the ole magazine of record. Yay, I suppose.

Vera is still having trouble sleeping, but she is getting better at it, I think. I bought this thing called a bagel (not the bread product) and it helps with feeding her. I put her in the bagel and rock her. I'll try to send you a picture. She looks very sweet and content.

Also I have some good news. I have met a lovely woman, several years my junior. I am not in love with her in the traditional sense, or at least in the way I was in love with your daughter, but I believe that she has fallen in love with me. She is a fan of my fledgling work and is herself well educated with a master's degree from Brown. More to the point, she (her name is Anne) has fallen in love with little Vera. And although, as a feminist, I would not wish maternity on anyone, I am surprised by the good fit we have together, the three of us.

I have thought a lot about what you said. About how your heart breaks just being in the same room as Vera. Her resemblance to her mother is uncanny. It's like I have no genes to give her at all (probably for the best). If you do not wish to see her right now, if you are <u>unable</u> to see her right now, I understand. And now you no longer have to worry about her and my lackluster parenting skills. Vera and I may have had a rocky beginning, but there is something that clicks in our family unit now that Anne has joined us. In ways I can't explain, even as a writer, seeing Anne be a full-fledged parent makes me want to emulate her, and as a result I love Vera more than I ever have. I really should send you a photo of that bagel.

Because of Anne, there is a lot of stability in our family. As it happens, Anne is not working at present and can devote all of her time to raising Vera. She has a little trust fund and together with my paltry salary, we make do. We are quite happy, in fact, which is not something I ever thought I would be after Iris passed. In time, we may give Vera a sibling or per-haps a pet.

I do not think there is anything "shameful" about the manner of Iris's passing, but I agree with you that, at least in her younger years, Vera should not know the circumstances of her mother's death, which she may well do if she is in direct contact with your family in Ohio.

And so, to use a horrible sports metaphor, I will leave the ball in your court. When you feel you are ready to see her, please write to me. Our goal should not be to deprive you of the joys of a granddaughter but to give Vera the most stable environment we can. Pursuant to that, we will celebrate her first birthday in Korean style with the pen and the arrows and all that, and she will take Korean lessons when she's older. Anne says she will buy her children's books that celebrate her Asian heritage. Apparently, there are very many to choose from. But, in general, it is important to position Anne as Vera's true mom in every sense, from the legal (see "trust fund" above) to the emotional to the—

For the first time in her life, Vera had stopped reading in the middle of something. She could read no longer. She could read no longer about herself in the third person. She did not want to exist as words on a document, words in a letter. She did not understand all of what she had read, but somehow she had to. It was like the ultimate final chapter of the *Things I Still Need to Know Diary*. It accounted for one hundred percent of the grade.

"Where is your father now?" Hun asked.

"He ran away to Budapest," Vera said. The words in her mouth felt dense and sour like Russian food.

"Ah."

"Your father was not ready to be a parent alone," Carol said. "And neither was our daughter before she went to heaven."

Vera nodded.

"But for ten years," Carol said, "your father tried to raise you with Anne."

"He lasted longer than we ever thought he would," Hun said. "Even as we read his letter, we thought, He writes beautifully, but he is lying. He will not be able to fulfill his duties."

Carol made a shushing sound. "We told him we would raise you, make his life easy, but he said no, he had to do it himself. He was your father."

"He chose this Anne to take care of you," Hun said. "And I think she has done a good job."

Vera put her head down into the elbow of her arm. If these were to be her grandparents, they would have to get used to the sound of a young girl crying. She felt her shoulders shake "spasmodically" as her grandmother's hand found her spine and massaged it gently over and over again while muttering something in Korean, the clipped ends of soft consonants and vowels falling out of her mouth like the rain.

"Why didn't you write to him?" she mumbled into her elbow, the "Octagon" elbow that could have used a fraternal punch right about now. "Why didn't you want to be my grandparents?" But she knew the answer. Not everyone could handle the pain of the world. It was like the religious ladies outside her school had written on their placards: WILL SUFFERING END? For some, it just couldn't.

"Why didn't you at least give me a Korean name?" she finally said out loud.

"We wanted to," Hun said. "Vera is very hard for us to pronounce."

"But my father talked you out of it," Vera said. "They say he can talk the pants off of anyone."

"No," Hun said. "This was your mother's idea. She

loved the name. The wife of her favorite Russian writer was named that. A wife who was a genius herself, but in the olden times she had to serve her husband."

This was a surprise to Vera. "My mother named me?" she said. "She named me 'faith'?"

"Vera," her grandmother said after a while. "We need to call your mother and tell her that you're okay. She must be so worried."

"Oh," Vera said, trying to remember who her mother really was. "Right."

,

Every minute before Anne Mom came had to count. Luckily, there was a large distance between Ohio and the city, even if one took a plane. Now that her grandparents had told her, more or less, how her mother had passed away, they couldn't stop speaking, as if, with their speech, they could make up for the terrible thing they had told her, as if, with their speech, they could bring Iris Choi back from the dead, back to her "facility," then back to Vera's father and the life they could have had if both of her birth parents had been different.

Vera was the world's best recorder, better than Kaspie even, and she recorded everything her grandparents told her. The capital of Jeolla Province where her ancestry hailed from was called Gwangju. In 1980 there was a rebellion there against "the dictatorship" and her family had something to do with it. Maybe they were heroes after all, even though her father always said there was no such thing as a hero, everyone did things for a reason and then history took all those reasons together and made a "giant pointless turd" out of it all. Her grandfather had gone to the local university, but it was hard for anyone from Jeolla Province to get ahead in Korea, especially during the dictatorship, but also kind of after the dictatorship, too. "I flew over Gwangju on the way from Seoul to Jeju Island," Vera said. "I saw it on the map!"

"Good girl," her grandmother said.

Her family moved to a place called Orange County ("Are there really oranges there?" methodic Vera wanted to know), where her grandparents tried a number of businesses that did not succeed. It was very hard for Vera's mother because they were not rich or white and in Orange County it was necessary to be one or the other back in those days. "Was she also a sad child?" Vera asked. The answer was yes. "Then I must have gotten my funny side from my father," she said.

Hun had trained as an engineer back in Korea, and through a network of his countrymen, he found a job with a famous company that made tires in Akron and the whole family moved to Ohio. There the family's situation improved, though life was still very hard for Vera's mother, but less so for her younger sister, who did not "take things to heart" as much. "I have a younger brother like that, too," Vera said. "Apple doesn't fall far from the tree, I guess."

Things got worse when her mom went to the College of Fading Repute. Her sadness increased. "I blame that college for everything," Carol said. "I know maybe it is irrational."

"Like meeting my father?" Vera said. "But then how could I have been born?"

"You have very sound reasoning," Hun said. "Maybe one day you will be an engineer like me."

"I will be a woman in STEM." Vera explained her pathway to Swarthmore. She hoped that her father still had connections to "pull" for her and her Colgate-bound brother from as far away as Budapest.

9

After a few hours of nonstop talking, Vera felt that she had exhausted her grandparents. They must have been in their eighties by now, and they lacked the angry vitality of her Russian grandparents. She did not want their hearts to overbeat and explode. Eventually, Carol yawned and said she would go into the living room and take a nap on the couch with the plastic cover. She put a worsted blanket over herself and immediately fell asleep, her glasses still on the bridge of her nose.

Vera had introduced Hun to Kaspie, and her grandfather was very happy with the chessboard. Soon, they were talking to each other loudly in Korean as the pieces glided across the board and Hun lost in a variety of ways. "Very clever guy," he would mutter in English sometimes about his new friend. "But chess is easier than *baduk,* or 'go' in English. I ask him to play *baduk,* but he says he is just a chessboard." Before she left, she would give Kaspie as a gift to her grandfather. Maybe he needed an extra companion. Now that she had Yumi, she would not be alone.

The day continued in this vein, quietly and lazily and perfectly. The only disturbance, just as the sun began to slip into a nearby Great Lake, was a helicopter flying very close by. Hun looked up, as if he could see it through the ceiling.

The noise must have woken Carol up. "Are you still hungry?" she asked, yawning. "Did you have enough to eat?"

Vera surprised herself by saying, "No," which might have been impolite.

"What can I make for you?"

"More *galbi-jjim,* please."

Her grandmother put her arms around her. She smelled like citrus and garlic and some kind of medicinal patch and Vera thought all those smells were great together and she would remember them as much as she would remember anything else her grandparents had said or done or cooked the first time she met them.

The table was set with great "alacrity" by both grandparents. A bowl that might as well have been a tureen was placed in front of Vera, smoking with the pleasant aromas of a dish first made thousands of miles away. Nobody was playing with him, but still Kaspie jabbered away in Korean, the language he had been missing all along.

"I would like to say a prayer," Hun said. The helicopter was now so near, he had to speak up.

And then the world exploded around them.

23.

She Had To

"Hands! Hands! I want to see hands!"

The men were wearing what looked like the armor she had seen in the Tokyo National Museum, black and glossy and slightly like a bug's. The glass of the sliding door leading out to the back porch had exploded. They heard the inner front door disconnect from its frame and saw it slide down the corridor and through most of the living room. The helicopter sounded like it was sitting on top of the house now.

They all had their hands raised, but the men in armor came straight for her grandparents and twisted them onto the floor. Vera heard them shout out in pain.

"No!" she shouted. "Leave them alone!"

But they were twisting their arms behind them and putting what looked like plastic strings behind their backs. The room filled with the chatter of radios. Grandma Carol was screaming terribly now. "No!" Vera shouted again.

"They're my grandparents." Nobody listened to her. Nobody took her seriously. Someone had placed his hands on her shoulders firmly enough that she couldn't wriggle out. She smelled metal, like summer sweat, but maybe it was just the armor. "Please leave them alone," Vera shouted, but she had run out of voice and now it was almost a statement.

She was surrounded by the armed men and she saw the words HUMAN TRAFFICKING RAPID RESPONSE written on them. HTRR, she thought. HITTER. HIT HER. She kept screaming about her grandparents, about poor Grandma Carol in such pain, but she did not have the right statuses to unlock the situation.

"You're okay, honey," a male voice was saying behind her. "You're okay now. We're going to take you to a safe place."

They were going to take her to a special facility like her mother. "No!" Vera shouted, summoning her last reserves of strength and breath. She was in a dream. Just like the dreams she usually had after she would see a MOTH. But when had the dream started? Had meeting her grandparents also been a dream? Had the drive to Ohio been a dream? Her "triumphant" friendship with Yumi? The whole school year?

No, it was all real. Only she was inside the MOTH now. She was in the middle of the parade. These were the MOTH people and they would now do to her and her grandparents what they had always wanted to do. She did not have Five-Three. She couldn't laugh at them the way Dylan had. It was like Anne Mom's speech to the activists and the women in ballet flats. "We thought that the pain of what was happening in this country wouldn't come to our doorstep. But it has." And it had. They were there now. They were past the doorstep.

She heard another male voice: "Stella! Where's Stella?"

"Do you know where Stella is?" the man who was holding her shoulders asked.

"Stella's my car!" Vera shouted. Something seemed to change in the room as she said it.

"Stella Bradford-Schmuck-something is your car?" one of the armored men asked.

"Complainant may be a car," she heard an officer say into a radio. Her grandmother was sobbing and her grandfather was saying something to her in Korean. And then everything changed once again.

9

Anne Mom was running through the space where the front door had been, through the living room and toward the kitchen. A dozen long guns were pointed at her immediately. "Don't you touch my daughter!" her mother was screaming.

"Ma'am, stop!" the armored men were shouting.

"Ma'am, we *will* shoot!"

"Mommy! Mommy! Mommy!" The *M* word came out of Vera's mouth and it wouldn't stop coming out. Her mother did not care about the guns and ran toward her, pushing aside the men in armor who held her. They clasped each other's arms in the middle of the kitchen and suddenly she was held in place and the spinning world was locked out.

"Mommy! Mommy! Mommy!" she shouted. She was crying and shouting at the same time.

"Ma'am," one of the officers was saying. "Do you have any proof of your relationship to this child? Any documentation?"

"I have to—" Vera said. "I have to—"

"What?" Mommy said. "What do you have to?"

She had to hold the family together. She had to survive recess. She had to get through the March of the Hated. She had to enjoy the brief time she had with Aunt Cecile. She had to fall asleep. She had to submerge the big secret deep inside her to get through the day. She had to keep Daddy and the Seal company. She had to survive the revenge of Miss Campari. She had to kiss Aunt Cecile. She had to be cool in front of Yumi. She had to survive Anne Mom's political thing. She had to survive the night. She had to spy on Daddy to figure out what was going on. She had to expand her *Things I Still Need to Know Diary.*

She had to visit Baba Tanya and Grandpa Boris in the suburbs. She had to figure out if Daddy was a traitor. She had to win the debate with Stephen. She had to tell Anne Mom the truth. She had to "hatch a plan." She had to make it to Ohio. She had to find out the truth about Mom Mom. She had to find out the truth about her mother and her father. She had to—

"I have to—"

She was crying in Mommy's arms, and the smell of Mommy, though not the smell of her grandmother, was her own smell, too, the smell she had known since she was an "unplanned" baby in this woman's arms. She saw her father's letter before her: "More to the point, she has fallen in love with little Vera." It was true, wasn't it? Her mommy had fallen in love with her.

"Ma'am, a birth certificate, even from a non–Cycle Through state, will do," one of the officers was saying, his tone now desperately conciliatory.

"Will you please let those poor people go!" Anne shouted, and something about her appearance and maybe the status in her voice made things happen around them very quickly, and Vera's grandparents were unshackled and now Grandma Carol was crying in Grandpa Hun's arms just as Vera was crying in Mommy's.

"I have to tell you something," Vera said.

"You don't have to tell me anything now," Mommy was saying. "We have to go home. We need to go home."

"I got a C on an English language arts test," Vera whispered into Mommy's pale, beautiful neck as she clutched her non-waist.

"It doesn't matter," Mommy was saying.

"I got a C and I ran away."

"It doesn't matter," Mommy kept saying.

"What matters then?"

"I don't know, honey," Mommy said. She tried to move off the kitchen floor, but her daughter was deadweight in her arms.

I am the meat between the buns, Vera thought. Even though my father is gone, I am the meat between the buns.

"Where is Dylan?" she asked.

"Aunt Cecile is watching him."

"When will Aunt Cecile die? How much more time do I have with her?"

"I don't know, my love," Mommy said. "There are so many things I just don't know." Now she was the one who was crying. "Is that why you don't love me?" she said. "Because unlike your father I don't even pretend to know?"

"No!" Vera shouted. "I love you! I love you, Mommy!"

All of the words wanted to come out of her now. All the long, special words that had been stored in her. What if her father was wrong, and change was possible? And a better life could be "around the corner" for her? A better life with grandparents and an aunt and an uncle with a ginger

Gary Shteyngart

beard and her new cousins, with Dylan and his little boy's nonsense, and a Mommy who loved her and would run past a dozen rifles to get to her, would probably run through a "volley" of bullets to throw her arms around her and protect her from all this world had in store for a little girl like Vera? And even if it were a life without her father and, eventually, without Aunt Cecile, it would be a life where both of them lived on, one as a faraway "Hungarian," the other as a spirit in her atriums and ventricles.

"We think it's the mother, we just need a confirmation," one of the armored men was saying into his radio. "Yes, complainant was a car. Three females, possibly one reproductive, we can run a Holmes on them."

Vera and Mommy got up from the floor. Around them was the detritus of an American house overturned. There was a broken painting of an American Jesus tending to a flock of American lambs. There was an American air conditioner wasting American energy on a day that it could have been turned off without anyone noticing. There were the scattered photographs of a middle-aged American couple, one Asian, one ginger, with their three American children. There was the shattered photograph of a fallen American in a graduation gown. There was an old American woman crying in two languages while being held and comforted by an old American tire engineer. And on the floor next to American Vera and her American Mommy, there was an overturned American bowl of American *galbi-jjim.*

Mommy took Vera by the shoulders and looked down and into her eyes. "I have to—" Vera started to say.

But Mommy wouldn't let her finish. "What do you have to?"

"I have to—"

"You're only ten," she said. Her voice was a mother's voice and it would brook no argument.

"You're only ten," she said.

Vera thought about it. Ten was a number and she was good with numbers, no matter what Miss Campari said. So, I'm only ten, she thought to herself. And then she imagined her future self, a middle-school Vera, a high-school Vera, a college Vera, a girlfriend Vera, a woman-in-STEM Vera, a mommy Vera, all looking back at this ten-year-old present-day, present-second Vera with all the pity and wonder and faith that older people needed to just get through the rest of their lives.

"I'm only ten," she repeated. It was what her mother wanted to hear and just maybe it was true.

Acknowledgments

Once again, my thanks and admiration flow like vodka at a Russian funeral in the general direction of my brilliant editor, David Ebershoff, and my supreme agent, Denise Shannon. Thank you for keeping me well edited and solvent. And thank you to everyone at Random House, including Maria Braeckel, Denise Cronin, Windy Dorresteyn, Luke Epplin, Ben Greenberg, Rachel Kind, Carrie Neill, Alison Rich, Andy Ward, and Maddie Woda.

So many people pitched in and helped educate me as I weaved my way through many versions of this book. They include (but are not limited to): Daisy Alioto, Alexis Cheung, Mary Childs, Douglas Choi, Neill Chriss, Jesse Drucker, Lisa Goldstein, Peter S. Goodman, Jeff Jarvis, May Jeong, Ariel Kaminer, and Jordana Narin.

A line in this book was stolen from my friend and mentor Chang-rae Lee's novel *Native Speaker*. See if you can guess which one!

About the Author

GARY SHTEYNGART was born in Leningrad in 1972 and came to the United States seven years later. His debut novel, *The Russian Debutante's Handbook,* won the Stephen Crane Award for First Fiction and the National Jewish Book Award for Fiction. His second novel, *Absurdistan,* was named one of the 10 Best Books of the Year by *The New York Times Book Review.* His novel *Super Sad True Love Story* won the Bollinger Everyman Wodehouse Prize and became one of the most iconic novels of the decade. His memoir, *Little Failure,* was a National Book Critics Circle Award finalist, and his novel *Our Country Friends* was a *New York Times* bestseller. His books have been published in thirty countries. He lives in New York City with his wife and son.

X: @Shteyngart
Instagram: @Shteyngart

About the Type

This book was set in Galliard, a typeface designed in 1978 by Matthew Carter (b. 1937) for the Mergenthaler Linotype Company. Galliard is based on the sixteenth-century typefaces of Robert Granjon (1513–89).